A CONFERENCE IN STOCKHOLM

By

Kathy Harter

This is entirely a work of fiction. Any resemblance to an actual person is purely coincidental. Some locations are accurate, some are fictionalized to avoid intrusion of privacy.

Highlights

Stockholm Series, Book I

A woman whose comfortable life is destroyed when her father is jailed for a Ponzi scheme is recruited into the C.I.A. Her early success leads to partnering with a legendary agent and after a rocky start they become a top team.

A renowned Russian dissident now living and teaching environmental science in Oxford, UK, is scheduled to give a speech on global warming and the resultant destruction at the Global Environmental Responsibility Forum in Stockholm, Sweden. Rumors abound that he will be naming names of greedy despots and corporate entities who want him stopped by any means necessary.

Past crimes by a member of the current administration have been uncovered. When it all goes wrong it becomes clear it was a setup and the two events are connected but who was the target and why?

Untangling it all means Joshua Daine and Valerie Rhodes must confront past demons and reach out before it's too late.

\#   \#

A Conference in Stockholm in the first in a trilogy of Joshua Daine and Valerie Rhodes books. *A House In Stockholm* is the second and *A Meeting in Stockholm* will be out later this year.

Other books by Kathy Harter

Fame Can Be Murder
Mac's Wife
El Conejo Rides Again
Brothers in Name Only
Divorce, Hollywood Style

Chapter 1

The embassy party in a small Eastern European capital was a dreary affair, primarily consisting of overdressed middle-aged middle-level civil servants. It was an annual event, to say thank you to all those who were of service during the year, in big and small ways. The U.S. ambassador gamely greeted all by name with a personal thank you; his wife was less dutiful and suffered through the night miffed that her husband, after all his donations to the new president, was stuck in this depressing outpost. It was all she could do to hide her irritation.

Adding to her day's woes, as she was dressing, a messenger had delivered a package not an hour before the festivities and she'd had to walk it upstairs to her husband's office herself. It was marked important and the servants were given time off to dress and he was in the shower.

Across the room, another woman much younger and prettier, wearing an off the rack loose fitting forest green sheath appeared to be having a great time. Her dance partner, a plump but game minion of the city government had, for a price, given valuable information to her boss who had dispatched her to pick up that small delivered package, an urgent last minute assignment that could not wait for the diplomatic pouch.

Smiling and implying that wonders were to come she sashayed him to a servant's door beyond the kitchen area leading to the back stairs. He passed her a key then helped himself to a tray of little sausages. She quickly rushed up the steps, her smile gone. At the top she counted one two three doors on the left and used the key to open the door.

Visible in the dim hall light, clearly with the same orders, stood the ambassador's male secretary. Double dealing, hardly a surprise. He was holding the small package in his left hand. The gun in his right hand spoke to his intent.

"Stand over there." He waved his gun towards the wall as he moved to shut the door.

"I believe that's intended for me," she said, as she instead moved towards the center of the room.

"I do not." Instinctively, confident with the gun, he took a threatening step closer.

Faster than he could react she sidestepped, jammed the flat of her hand into his nose with a follow up kick to the groin. She grabbed the package before it hit the ground while he flailed up then down in pain. She ran to the open French doors onto a small balcony and quickly stepped over the railing onto an ivy covered trellis. Unfortunately it was a rotting trellis, down she went onto a window canopy that slowed a harsher landing into a row of bushes.

"Oomph."

Scratched and slightly limping she shoved the small package down her cleavage between the foam pads she'd added for effect. At the curb a valet was coveting a small sports car as he opened the door for the owner, uninterested in a disturbance behind him.

Before either realized what had happened she hopped in and roared off. From the window above the man realized he had no shot and would only disturb the party. He pulled out his phone.

A country or so over, in a luxury hotel bar, sat an attractive man in a tux, sipping a drink, back to the wall in a darkened corner. He appeared to be casually watching the other patrons, maybe waiting for someone, maybe waiting for something to happen. No one paid him much notice, the hotel was new, rumored to be owned by a wealthy sheikh in Dubai. Famously connected people were paid to patronize their establishments; many a minor royal survived on such handouts.

Sashaying directly to the bar, an attractive blond, wearing a bright red low cut designer gown, accepted an offered drink. Every bar from there to Shanghai was stocked with arm candy for the well healed.

He continued sipping his drink, ordered another, this time leaving out his AmEx black card to run a tab. That got her attention. With barely a nod she left her drink, walked across and sat at his table. He signaled the bartender, bring the lady another drink. She reached across to touch his hand.

A short time later the two exited the elevator, no air between them. He opened the door to his luxury suite, romantic moonlight through the curtains. Still locked in his embrace, she began immediately unbuttoning his shirt while he pulled the tie, then turned so he could he unzip her, each garment removed a step closer to the bed. Not bothering to remove the comforter the two bodies intertwined to inner music each could hear.

Until the music was a phone that buzzed from his jacket, on the floor.

"Ignore that, darling. I'll make it worth your while."

Not bothering to say "excuse me," he slipped from her arms to retrieve the phone. His companion looked like the dog just ate her winning lottery ticket.

"Day off mean anything?" He used an earpiece, gathering his clothes and dressing while he listened then disconnected. At the door he turned.

"Oh, I almost forgot." He picked up her dress from the floor and moved to hand it to her. Instead, he reached inside, found a hidden pocket, held up his credit card.

"You can spend a lot of money before a happy man wakes up." Her expression hardened.

"Enjoy the room, it's paid for."

Downstairs at the front desk, he handed over the card. "She's still in the room, if you want her."

"It's enough we have her picture." He pointed to a camera, at the bar entrance. "I'll circulate to the other hotels, put her out of business. Far worse than a few days in jail, I assure you. Stay for dinner, talk old times? I owe you one."

"One?" He laughed. "But no, thanks, can't stay. My day job called."

#   #

The spring day after a gray winter meant streets in the small village outside Prague were jammed with bargain hunting vacationers, eager to look behind the iron curtain without touching. Citizens previously under the communist umbrella had recently discovered the capitalistic benefits of tourism; little sidewalk cafes, like a Las Vegas Parisian trompe l'oeil, dotted the street. A visit to Paris without the cost and well, the French.

Valerie Rhodes, looking far different from the woman that had made her escape from the embassy a few days before mixed with a group of tourists, feeling the love of wearing a beret as she strolled happily along, hands full of shopping bags. She wore dark glasses against the bright sun, her light brown hair was tied behind her and her cotton pants were slightly baggy and a little wrinkled, topped by a tee shirt with an Italian designer logo.

Casually so as to not draw attention she slowed in front of a window selling resort wear, appearing to eye the prices but her expression changed to watchful as she checked the reflection for anything behind her. She studied each piece as she looked both ways. Nothing disturbed her and she continued cheerfully down the street, gradually putting distance between herself and the tour. No one seemed to notice.

At a cafe called *Il Jovia* she adjusted her packages to open the rustic door.

The space was larger than it appeared from the front, with extra seating along the alcove to the kitchen. There were booths along one wall and sturdy wooden tables in the center, filled with enough diners to trust the food. Decorated like an English pub, with the ubiquitous sturdy bar dominating, logo plaques touting fine British ale and a dart board, never used, displayed in contrast to the Italian name and French menu posted in the

9

window as if to welcome all wanting the continental experience.

She removed the glasses, adjusting her eyes as she scanned the room. Several lone patrons ate with book in hand, a young couple with eyes only for each other and across the room a small gathering enjoying a celebration. Sitting at a side table, again back to wall facing the door, was a slightly impatient man wearing a plaid shirt, well worn jeans and a light cotton jacket. Her expression noted she'd found her man.

Joshua Daine, the man whose hotel assignation was derailed now looked like every married man waiting for his wife, the coffee cup at his elbow nearly empty. Daylight showed signs of age around the eyes and in a sprinkling of gray in his uncombed longish dark blond hair. Finally, his body language seemed to say before he smiled, careful that his blue eyes avoided signs of irritation.

The waiter, Franz from the tag on his red vest, had seen that look often. A man must always wait for his wife, it was a rule as much as choosing a mistress from another city. Two waiters were on duty, trying not to appear rushed, both thrilled to have American customers, they tipped better than Europeans. Especially locals who hated to part with even the cost of the meal.

Valerie breathlessly rushed to the table, said "'scuse me" over her shoulder when one of her bags touched another diner. She set the bags on the floor next to her chair as she slid in, obviously happy to see him. The woman in the corner who'd been eyeing him over the rim of her book frowned when she saw he was no longer alone. Franz quickly snagged the couple; the other waiter glared, perhaps he could steal part of the tip later.

"Coffee, madam?"

She smiled the bright smile of a happy woman with her man. "A mocha latte, almond milk, no foam, a brush of cinnamon, that would be perfect, thank you." Franz had no idea what that meant but nodded. To Joshua, she said, "Sorry I'm late, darling. There's just so much to see. And buy."

"You're here now and that's what matters. Foreign countries, I worry about you, sweetheart, you know that." The edge in his voice was hard to pick up but her expression shifted slightly. A heavy set woman, tray laden with cakes and pastries, passed by.

She pointed. "I'd like one of those layered cakes with the….. oh, I almost forgot, I bought you something." She bent to retrieve something in one of the bags losing her beret in the process.

Joshua signaled Franz. "Another coffee. And a Napoleon."

Franz nodded and disappeared. Joshua leaned in as if to steal a kiss. His voice, however, was quietly cold and cutting. "What the hell took you so long?"

Nuzzling his neck slightly, she said, "Tourists. They stop to take pictures of every damn bird dropping but it was the best cover I could find."

"The importance of time is….."

"Synchronizing watches went out even before your legendary heyday."

Franz arrived with their order. Each replaced their happy to be together expression.

He moved aside to place her coffee, black, on the table as Valerie looked up. Simultaneously the waiter behind him turned from taking an order, giving her a clear view into the kitchen. Staring back, eyes wide, bandage across his nose was the man from the embassy, wearing an apron.

She cut him off. "We've got to get out of here....now...." She moved to gather up her packages. The man threw off his apron as he charged out of the kitchen, gun in hand. The surprised waiter nearest the door inadvertently bumped the shooter's arm and the shot went through the front window. Without hesitation, Franz, near the counter, did not duck for cover but also pulled a gun hidden beneath his apron and turned to get his clear shot.

The woman still watching Joshua screamed. The calm demeanor was shattered by the second gunshot that also missed it's target as the man at the table behind jumped up, in the process again knocking the gunman's arm. Other diners dove for cover. Joshua quickly overturned their table, grabbed his gun from behind his belt and returned fire. Valerie, too, pulled a gun and crouched to return fire. One of the lone diners dropped his book and pulled out a gun. Four guns were firing simultaneously as patrons ran or screamed.

"Does the word 'clandestine' mean anything to you?" He fired.

"Me? You're supposed to clear rendezvous points." She fired.

"It was clear until the waiter recognized you." They both fired.

"I didn't choose a meeting place with so many spies that the bathroom has a vending machine selling fake passports." She fired, hitting another gunman in the leg. He went down, his bullet into the ceiling.

Each fired a few rounds then ducked as gunfire was returned. Bullets were pinging everywhere. The owner, behind the counter, was terrified and livid at the destruction. The owner's wife, moving the pastry tray to safety, yelled at all as she grabbed a still hot fry pan and screamed at them to get out. She hadn't left war torn Bosnia to let her cafe be ruined. The swinging pan caused another shot to go wild as the blow's recipient grabbed his seared arm.

"Shoot your stupid bullets at Rosa's down the street, it's a slop house. No one would notice a bullet in her pies!" Like an oversized floral attired ninja with a nunchuck she swung the heavy iron frying pan at anyone foolish enough be be in her sight line.

Joshua used the interruption to grab Valerie and head for the door. "What the hell, two days off and you start a war?"

"That 'waiter' was waiting at the embassy pickup."

"Next time you wander off to make new friends, let me know." He fired, hitting the other waiter in the shoulder, who dropped his gun. "I'll bring extra ammo."

"Behind you, two more." They both fired, gaining enough time to flee out the door where the street had emptied.

"Where's your car?"

"A rental, too easy to trace. Follow me."

Sirens, gradually louder, blared in the background. "Wait, my…." She moved to retrieve her packages but he yanked her away. They ran quickly, keeping low, into the now deserted street as the first police car drove up. Joshua waved his arms, frantically, as if in distress. The cop didn't buy it and nearly ran him down as he jumped aside. But the cop's face froze as he saw Valerie, in front of the car, a very intent expression on her face and her gun pointed at his head. He slammed the brakes to a stop, inches from her. Joshua pulled the officer from the car, got behind the wheel as Valerie jumped in the back seat seconds before he sped off, siren still bleating.

"Fucking A...." He found the knob to turn it off.

Loudly, as she pulled herself from the floor, she said, "Ouch. Don't mind me." She rubbed her shoulder. "Just another panther like escape from the great Joshua Daine."

"Panic out of H.Q., find you and get you out of Dodge, fast, with the computer intel. You still haven't told me why you're even here. Last thing you said was off to Paris."

Minutes later, the tiny blue and white police car bounced at a higher than recommended speed along an unpaved country lane. She attempted to climb into the front seat while he maneuvered the steering wheel. She narrowly avoided hitting her head on the roof.

"You don't win a prize for banging every pothole, you know." She fell more than slid onto the front, managed to get upright. "Just get me back to headquarters for a new assignment."

"You might want to give some thought to getting out of this one first."

He turned his head to her for emphasis, nearly missing a sharp turn in the road. Just in time he swerved the car only to see a small herd of cows blocking the road.

"Look out!" She leaned over and grabbed the wheel, jerking it sideways. They missed the cows but the car made a bumpy landing in a water filled ditch, and stalled. They got out, to stare at their predicament.

"Give me your phone."

"What? No, I'm calling for a ride."

"The first time it's turned on, we're toast, might as well resist temptation. We'll pick up new, a town just over there. I know a guy." He held out his hand.

"You always know a guy. Now would be a good time for that guy."

She handed it over. He pulled his from a pocket and stomped on both. "There's probably a tracker on the car so we don't have much time."

The look she gave him was murderous but he was already moving. She had no choice but to follow.

# #

Back at the cafe, it was remarkably calm after the chaos. It was a city that had been through a lot over the years. The patrons had all disappeared; the owner and his wife sat at one of their tables. He was resigned, she was scowling. Few were on the street outside, their curiosity having taken a back seat to getting involved. The police officer, no doubt postponing when he had to report his stolen car, walked around and surveyed the damage, taking copious notes. He didn't notice or chose to not notice Franz the waiter and only one left, through the small window to the kitchen.

Franz rifled through the packages Valerie had brought to the cafe that he'd been quick enough to grab in the chaos as he held a phone to his ear.

On the other end of the phone was an attractive woman, in her forties at least with the high maintenance gloss of salon blond and well dressed in a western style but through the window were the onion domes of the Kremlin. Her apartment was lavish; everything about her screamed trophy wife to a Russian oligarch except her voice; a woman used to getting her own way.

"Do you have it?"

"Do not insult me. Just send the money."

In the background a once good looking man sat at the table, still with remains of a meal, sipping vodka, watching her carefully. He had an air of importance, stylish gray hair and wore expensive jogging clothes. Besides early signs of aging badly the only thing that marred his looks was a slight indent just below the bridge of his nose yet it also added character to his what could have been, in his youth, a too pretty face. Women were drawn to it, at once curious and turned on by this flaw.

While she talked she strolled across to sit on his lap. He began to unbutton her blouse as she smiled. Her softness of movement belied her cold voice.

"Were there any problems? Did anyone recognize you?"

"Of course not. It's done, exactly as planned. I will expect the rest of the payment." He disconnected the phone, not happy. He thought a few moments then dialed his phone. When answered he said, with urgency,

"You had better find them. And fast. No excuses this time."

At the apartment, the man began kissing her as he moved his hand inside her blouse. He said, firmly, "You must make one more call, darling, one more, as I explained. Did you learn what I told you?"

"Yes, I am not stupid."

"Of course not, my darlin'. Make your call. Then I am all yours. When is your husband returnin'?" His accent was decidedly American with a slight southern inflection.

She giggled and dialed the phone.

"Hello? Hello, my darling Papa? I have such a wonderful surprise for you. I cannot wait to tell you."

# #

Near sunset the two weary travelers spotted a wooded area with a farmhouse in the distance. It looked deserted but then lights popped on in the kitchen. Valerie pointed to the barn, far enough away and days work done, where they could stop to rest and figure out their options.

"We sleep in the woods."

She was not at all pleased, a simple plan gone awry. They had trudged through unfamiliar back country to evade captors who no doubt had brought in reinforcements to search for them. Lived on the edge, his reputation from getting out of tight spots that were due, in her mind, to his reckless planning. A light drizzle began to dampen the air along with her spirits.

"A barn has hay and a roof. You can stand watch." She started to head down.

He grabbed her arm. "We rest there. It's safer." He pointed to a rise above the barn where trees and new underbrush would hide them. Small comfort, she thought, frowning, the trees would block the rain.

Ignoring her he shoved aside some brush and within minutes had fixed up an almost cozy spot under a shrub. She stared, nonplussed.

"If you're looking for a compliment on your Boy Scout skills, I don't consider a bush qualified as a B and B."

"It will have to do. I prefer night travel but the rain will leave footprints and we need to see where we step."

"Gee, if only I'd brought my size 12 work boots we could fool them. Is that your best exit strategy? I was kind of hoping for one that worked this time."

"That's tomorrow's problem. Now we need rest to be out of here, that farmer will be up before daylight. Lousy job, ask me."

"Sure, much worse than ours."

He was unsure of her mood but he was sure of their danger. He grabbed her by the shoulders. "I'll get you out of this, I promise."

She hadn't expected that. "Right. Okay, then, you can have the computer stick." She reached inside her blouse and pulled out a small blob of packing tape, handed it to him. "It's scratchy anyway."

He stared at it. "Are you sure something is in there?"

"Orders to pick up at the embassy. Leap of faith trusting that source, man with gun problem, now it's your problem."

"It'll have to wait." He slipped it into a sealed inner pants pocket. "Why were you there alone?"

"Last minute rush job."

"I meant why just you? I should've run backup."

"How the hell to do I know? We take orders, came from top, Old Ironpants himself. I figured you were off somewhere. Besides, since when can't I do a simple grab and go without a minder?"

"That's not the point. Waiting for you at the embassy and at the cafe? It was an ambush."

She stared at him. The implications of that was not good news. A crack of thunder sounded in the distance. She almost jumped at the sound.

"What?"

"Nothing." She didn't add, middle of nowhere, men with gun problem.

"We rest a bit. I hear water over that rise, it will hide our tracks."

Too exhausted to argue, she crawled into the makeshift shelter, then made room for him. Instead he turned away. "You're not joining? When it's so artfully decorated?"

"I'll be over there, better vantage." He pointed back towards the road. "No reason to think we're in the clear." Before she could answer he'd disappeared.

An hour later, as night deepened, she woke from a fitful sleep, freezing. All the animals of the forest were silent, no doubt comfy in their nests. The rain had let up. A barn had hay and possibly blankets, she was sure she had heard a horse earlier. Quietly, so as to not disturb him on watch she crept out of the makeshift shelter and down the hill.

19

The barn was dark but the door wasn't locked and carefully she slipped inside. A horse whinnied softly; she moved to stroke its nose to calm it, a cow in another stall silently watched. Across was a makeshift office with the door ajar.

She stepped inside, saw an old mattress on the floor with blanket and pillow, neither looked clean enough to sleep on. As she reached for the blanket she noticed an old barn jacket hanging on a hook. She put it on, pleased as she felt some warmth.

Back at the wooded area Joshua went on alert. Off in the distance he heard a car, moving too fast. Quietly and quickly he hurried over to grab Valerie. Just as he realized the shelter was empty the car turned in, lights on the barn door. He watched as four heavily armed men ran in the front of the barn and began noisily banging on each stall.

He knew what was about to go very wrong; he ran down behind the barn, unconcerned if the dark offered enough cover.

Valerie had heard the car and ducked back into the office, her gun up and prepared for a fight. One of the gunman yelled something and before she could react she faced serious weaponry. One signaled her to hand over her gun and follow them. She complied, thinking it was no longer tomorrow's problem.

Joshua, hidden by the darkness behind the barn, knew the element of surprise would more likely get her killed in any exchange of gunfire. He'd risk it for himself but not for her. Alive, he could find her.

He needed to go, he couldn't delay. He ran, getting nearly to the shelter of trees when the first shots rang out. It was dark enough that their aim was bad but another car arrived and immediately men, better armed, jumped out and sprayed the area. He continued moving, fast and silent, into the woods. Just as he reached atop a ravine, preparing to jump down for cover, a bullet grazed his forehead. His body lurched then tumbled down the hillside into the cold estuary river. His body was pulled further by the current, ravaged by the recent rains and snowfall.

Two gunmen gathered at the top. A third arrived with a high voltage lantern he aimed until they saw his lifeless body floating along, face down. One of the gunman started to fire again but was stopped.

"Enough. Let's get out of here. He'll freeze in that water if he's not dead already. Pay off the old farmer to keep quiet. He heard nothing."

The first car had left and turned onto the roadway. Valerie, in the backseat, stared out the window, her expression one of dread.

Chapter 2

The shiny black Range Rover drove past a sign that said Oxford, 2 km, slowing as it exited the A4 onto Garlington Road and the beginning of morning commutes, past the outlying housing tracts. A mile or so further, shortly before crossing Magdalen Bridge that became High Street into city centre proper, the vehicle made a right turn into what appeared to be a clump of bushes behind a pub car park. The occupants were not visible behind the tinted windows as the vehicle maneuvered the even narrower lanes lined with attached row houses; speed was discouraged.

A light snow covered the ground but the sun promised to be a bright crisp day and would soon melt. A fox ran across the road, with blood sports out of favor the population was encroaching. Tourists who enjoyed the many parks, river banks and green spaces were not yet out, only a few joggers and a stroller pushed by a determined mum were the only movement. Another kilometer further into the Oxfordshire countryside the vehicle pulled behind a small cottage nearly hidden in foliage, common in a nation where no one left home without an umbrella, and stopped.

Rod Bernmeister, the driver, who looked every bit the mercenary he once was, stepped out. His eyes, hidden behind tinted glasses, quickly surveyed the landscape before opening the back door. Barely visible was another man in the front seat.

Bennett Daine, a tall, trim man with rigid posture and expression to match, stepped out from the back seat. He wore an expensive overcoat, open to show an equally bespoke tailored suit with muted silk tie and no hat, gloves or scarf that suggested he would never be long outdoors in bad weather.

"I might be a while if you'd like to wait in the pub we passed."

"That's all right, sir, we're fine. We'll do a perimeter check." Bernmeister was his longtime bodyguard and doubled as driver when his ability to get out of tight spots might be needed. Nigel Suffington also stepped out, his eyes watchful. He was a backup local hire they'd used before, ex-military, knocked out by shrapnel in the Gulf War but his shooting skills were top notch and he was smart.

Daine nodded. He paid top dollar for top help and they knew their job. His visit was supposed to be secret but in these days of heightened security little was, he knew, although he doubted anyone would risk an attack in such an isolated spot. A Range Rover on British motorways was hardly noticed. Trees might hide the cottage from sight but they were little help in an exit strategy, risky at best, although that did not always matter, only if identification was it a problem.

The door to the cottage opened and Yevgeny Yurovinsky, one eye partially covered by his unkempt shaggy dark hair now graying and a jovial smile on a well worn face, rushed outside. His body, in contrast to his well turned out guest, showed the wear and tear of a man used to the good life of food and drink. He wore baggy brown trousers and a worn buttoned green sweater over a black turtleneck. His apparent disinterest in appearance had become his image, a calculated absent minded professorial casual look that couldn't be further from reality.

"Bennett, *privye*t, I am grateful you can make time to visit an old man." Happily, he called out his greeting in Russian, encompassing him in a familiar bear hug as the old comrades and friends they were. Bennett laughed, he did not mind but clearly would have preferred a handshake.

"Yevi, my old friend, so good to see you." His accent was American but with traces of his long ago upbringing in London. "Always it seems too long. I only had to cancel a meeting rather hurriedly but they will no doubt appreciate time to discuss my position before accepting it as their own idea. You sounded urgent."

He held the door. "You always got the best of us. And not everyone realized it."

Inside, Daine removed his coat and hung it on the coat rack. He followed his host and took the offered vodka, held high, for a toast, "*Skål*," as was their familiar greeting. The two men in appearance were opposites. Bennett was in his sixties according to his official biography, gray hair immaculately styled, few wrinkles and a handsomely distinguished well cared for face that made him seem far younger than his friend.

"Sit, sit, sit, *starik*, welcome to my home." His beefy hand swirled to the cluttered room, filled with books and papers and many photos of a young woman in her twenties with dark hair. Two bookshelves lined one wall, a fireplace dominated another and a large window looked out on a small garden with several bare trees and just beyond a small structure with smoke from a chimney. He noticed Bennett looking at it.

"Do not worry. We can see out but no one can see in. There are sensors also. I am well protected. That little cottage lives a couple, both highly trained, although I suspect them of reporting back. Still, it is their job to keep me alive."

"And when it's not their job?"

Yurovinsky shrugged. "So many things to worry about, it cannot be that." He took another swig of vodka, offered another to Bennett who shook his head.

"So, Yevi, what is it you cannot tell me on the phone? And is it any safer here to speak? Could not you come to my flat in town?"

"I removed the listening devices, one learns many tricks over years of repression. They will no doubt return soon but for now we can talk. With you here in London for the economic summit to pretend the U.S. will lift sanctions in Russia, it would seem unusual for you not to visit."

"You want them to know we've spoken but not the topic?"

"You were always the one so sparse with words, *bratishka*." He laughed his deep laugh. "Since you were a boy you kept your thoughts to yourself. Speaking of boys, how is you son, Joshua. Is it better between you?"

"I'm afraid not. He blames me, of course, for his mother, for sending him away, for...." He shrugs. "We've barely spoken in years. He doesn't confide in me."

26

"I am sorry, my friend. He is your son, so many expectations of him even though he is a success in his own right. But sons, right? You must give him time. You were deprived of your father at a young age and found your way alone." He swept his arm to encompass the photos then raised his glass. "My daughter Lina, she blames me for nothing, even when she should." He laughed again, took a large sip, then turned serious. "But it is of her I wish to speak. Did you know I was invited to give a talk at the global climate conference in Stockholm in a few months?"

"I know of the conference, of course, and with your excellent work on climate accord I can't say I'm surprised. But there are also rumors that it might be more than just a gathering of scientists, that some more fervent groups wanting more immediate change might choose to be disruptive. I also know you well, my friend, that you may be planning to rattle some cages and not in a good way."

"It's true. I have decided to prepare a speech to blow the lid off, as you Americans say, on crimes the government has allowed against our future survival. The tie in to fossil fuel impact with remuneration to a few and the destruction of many."

"It will put you in great danger."

He waved it away. "I know this. But Bennett, I cannot speak only to students any longer and publish papers from my research. The time for polite documentation has passed. The young, they know this, they protest, but those in power now, it's been a concentrated effort in many countries to intercept elections and I don't mean always in legal ways by those who deny our future. They continue to ignore and even discontinue regulations...." He stopped, slightly chagrined, drank his vodka.

"My friend. Of course you know this. Sometimes I cannot help myself. But it's partly why I ask you for help. I need you to protect my Lina. She called me, we had not spoken in some time, it can still be risky for her. She insisted on being with me at the conference. I cannot stop her. She's like her mother in this, once her mind is made up...." He shook his head. "I know you have resources that can do this for me. I don't care about myself, it's been a good life, it cannot go on forever but my darling child, she has so much left. You can take her to America if anything happens to me. I know you can do this."

"Yes, I suppose I can and of course I will see that she's in good hands but it will be much safer to see you're well protected and to get her out before the speech..."

"It will not be possible, she is under heavy guard, to keep me in line. She said she can be there, in the audience or they will not let me speak. No, I've thought this through carefully. It must be done this way. Once I have spoken there will be confusion. I have friends who will see to it. That will be your chance to take her to safety. Do not worry about me. As I said, I have friends that will plan my escape but if it does not work..." He shrugs. "You are the one person in the world I trust to do this. Tell me you will honor my wish."

"Of course I will see to it. I owe you a great deal."

Yevi brushed that aside. "You owe me nothing but our lifelong friendship. And our mutual love of our children."

"But again, I caution you, it will be risky. Are you sure there is no other way?"

He lifted himself from the deep chair with a grunt and walked across the room to his cluttered desk, chortling as he said, "The best hiding place in the world, under piles of my beloved scientific research." He rummaged through the papers until he said, "Aha," and held up a manila envelope.

"Here are the plans, as much as I was able to learn in such a short time. I will no doubt learn more once all plans are in place."

"I will study them on the plane. But it would be good to talk before."

"Yes, yes, of course. Ah, now I hear birds fly off, they have noticed the absence of sound and set out their guard dogs. We can speak no more. Equipment today can do so much. Stay for lunch, we will laugh and toast to the good days, when as young men we were the scourge of our university tutors."

Both men raised their glasses in a hearty toast and headed for the kitchen where a feast of breads and cheeses and meats and drink awaited them on a large table. Through the window a flash of light, binoculars, the man behind invisible.

An hour later, remains of food eaten, Yurovinsky asked, "What do you mean you are thinking of retiring? And doing what?"

"The new administration, I cannot deal with them. No one can. It's time to let those with passion take up the fight. I've lost my energy for it. My colleagues have aged, as have I, some are already gone. The summit I'm attending was a last minute invite, from an old colleague."

Yevi laughed. "You are still the great Bennett Daine. Living up to that is a full time job. Even back in school, all the boys were in awe of you."

"Not you, surely."

"I was a poor foreign student, a young man barely speaking in English, on one of those goodwill scholarships your people arranged. I was terrified but you were my protector. I have never forgotten."

"You would have excelled without me. I could see that even if you couldn't. I had a plan. Your brain, I knew, would save a few of my grades." Both men laughed.

"Not in economics, my friend, not in economics."

"No. Not there. I've done well. As have you. You are a renowned scientist in your field, people have begun to listen." As he stood he could see out the front window, to Bernmeister's face. He didn't change his expression but knew it was a clear signal that it was time to go.

"One more toast and then I must rescue my team. It's getting chilly, even for them."

"Here. Give them a bottle of wine for later. They will forgive you."

Bennett raised his glass and nodded his thanks for the wine. The men walked to the door, shook hands and hugged as if unsure they would meet again.

"Goodbye my friend. Soon, I will be in touch…" He saw the car door was open and the motor running. With a familial nod at his friend, he quickly disengaged. If Yurovinsky noticed anything amiss he did not react.

Outwardly calm, not rushing, Daine handed over the envelope and wine to his driver then stepped inside the Range Rover. Bernmeister wasted no time shutting the door and handing over the materials to Suffington as he hopped in and sped off.

Without waiting until they reached the roadside pub, Suffington turned and said, "Sir. There was a call. Your son, he was reported missing. An assignment gone wrong."

"How wrong?"

"They reported he was killed, sir. I'm sorry. Shot. Near the Ukraine border."

Daine took a breath. "Cancel my appointments and take me to the embassy. I need a secure phone line. Do we still have contacts over there?"

"Already done, sir. They're waiting for instructions."

"His partner?"

"No word yet, sir."

The car turned onto the roadway. Bennett Daine stared straight ahead, his eyes darkened with fury, his mind focused as the car raced onto the motorway.

\#   \#

Chapter 3

Valerie sat rigidly upright, expressionless, in a small airless room that smelled of broken bodies and souls. Dark stains splotched the wall, blood had been spilled in here. One window, high up, let in a small beam of light. As they hadn't blindfolded her on the long uncomfortable drive, handcuffed to the back seat, she knew she was in a basement on the outskirts of *Usti nad Labem* in the Czech Republic.

She had sat, unattended, in a jail cell for almost a week. The guard that left food twice a day only looked at her to determine she was not close enough to do him harm. No one spoke to her, not a word or a threat but orders had come from somewhere as finally they had brought her directly to the barren room, consisting only of a marred table and four chairs. She still wore the barn jacket, which they searched thoroughly, now looking worse if possible but it's oversize gave her some comfort. She had no interest in pondering her fate, or her smell for that matter. Situations like this were rarely good; best to keep focused and a clear head, as much as was possible.

Every ounce of training went into not sinking into despair but she wasn't fooled, a prison was her best hope. She'd heard the gunfire but chose to believe that Joshua, true to his reputation, was alive and would find a way to bring her home. Whatever awaited her she held on to that, like a mantra meant to calm the spirit.

Knowing she was being watched through the one way glass pane in the wall she let her mind wander back to her first sight of Joshua Daine. His name was whispered among her training class, the rich man's son who joined the company, as the C.I.A. was called. The young men wanted to be him and the women, well, they wanted him. But for her, days of intense training were an exhausting blur and if she had any energy for musings it would have been that accepting the first job offered was a mistake. But forced to leave college by her father's betrayal, jailed for using his investors in a Ponzi scheme, what choices did she have?

She went through the motions for lack of any alternative. Soon, though, the physical workout improved her mood not to mention her body strength and she loved learning languages. She could move to Paris, her dream. Armed with an exciting new goal she began to really apply herself, soon becoming the top trainee.

And so after the mandatory six month course she asked for time to consider their offer intending to turn it down but not ready to cut the cord. She rarely went out drinking with the others, preferring to study which didn't endear her, and had managed to save some of her meager salary. Paris here I come, she cheerily sang off key, as she had packed.

She should have been suspicious when they'd readily agreed and even advanced her ticket cost but she was new to the ways of covert ops. Hardly covert, she had soon realized. She hadn't been there a week when they'd asked for "a simple thing, really, hardly even a favor." A branch of Danska Bank was suspected of funneling foreign payments to an American firm, part of a series of shell companies to avoid scrutiny. They had the American consultant under surveillance but without his contact they had no proof and no way to break the chain.

She was to get a job at the bank, conveniently an opening for a secretary to the assistant branch manager. Since she was fluent they'd done up a nice resume for her. Nothing sinister, just keep an eye out for any transactions that were slightly irregular. That would give them the contact.

Since they would be paying her in addition to the meager bank salary although, it was stressed, she would have to live on that. It suited, she would do the job, feel her way around and think about her future.

The girl at the next desk was named Juliette Fontaine. As it happened her roommate had run off with her boyfriend, leaving her stuck with rent she couldn't afford. She didn't want to move, it was walking distance to work and a lovely view, so difficult to find, she had tearfully explained. Valerie returned with her after work, saw it was a lot better than her dank one room. She gave Juliette half her share and said she'd pay the rest on payday.

Juliette was a decent cook, taught her how to buy the best produce late in day when prices dropped and knew all the resale clothing shops. She was tiny, had short dark hair and an upturned nose which she crinkled whenever something displeased her. The job was relatively easy, the bank manager was out more than in, took few calls, dictated few letters. She might have forgotten she had other business at hand until one day, when her boss was scheduled to be in but caught in a traffic pileup, a caller with a decidedly Russian accent had left a cryptic message about a package of dolls for his granddaughter. Her boss was gay, he had no children or their offspring.

At lunch, she begged off Juliette and left a message in the assigned spot with the exact time so they could trace the call. Likely a prepaid phone but would give them proof of their target.

A week later the bank was raided, all employees told to go home until further notice. Outside, on the sidewalk comforting Juliette, in tears about loss of her job, she saw him across the street, with and yet apart from the *gendarmes*. She wasn't sure why she'd recognized him, photos of covert agents weren't available but one of their instructors had met him and shared a few tantalizing details. It had been more than that, though, something about his aloofness and confidence, out of place in the excitement. If he had noticed her he gave no sign.

Because she had pegged him right off it was the first thing she'd mentioned when they met officially. He hadn't appreciated the helpful hint but she'd noticed he never again let himself be recognized so easily. She wondered how he'd stayed alive so long.

She was jolted out of her memories when two men entered. They took their time, saying nothing, ignoring her. They'd no doubt been watching her from behind the mirror opposite. She had refused to stare back into it; never show fear, they would never see that. The older one looked like a circus roustabout that had seen far better days. Behind him was his complete opposite, who looked more like a teaching assistant at a university. He sat across from her and set out a notebook without a glance in her direction

The room was so hot Valerie could smell the sweaty armpits of the interrogator who, no doubt to prove his alpha, paced around her. His face was the only soft part of him, gone to pudgy but showed no remorse or enthusiasm for what only he knew was to come. He was not tall but wide, all muscle. His small dark eyes, proportionally larger lower lip and flat nose made him ugly. He seemed to use it as a weapon, as if in repulsion to his looks she would spill all. She also knew he would kill her where she sat at a nod from the other one, who took notes but otherwise continued to show no interest.

He spoke, in better English than she would have guessed, accented but understandable. "We know you were not alone. Your partner, though, is the one we want. Tell us where he is and you will go free. You are extra but we will keep you unless we get something in return. If not, who knows, your pretty face might not be so pretty." He had the voice and stained fingers and teeth of a heavy smoker. In another time and place she could simply outlive him.

If he expected her to blurt out anything he would be disappointed. She had no interest in talking. If this were her last day on earth she would not give him an ounce of satisfaction. Whatever that creature said she knew Joshua would never betray her and she had no intention of bargaining, as if for one minute she thought they would keep their word. Did they not realize it was Interrogation 101?

Before he could conjure up a better threat, the door opened and a well dressed man with a thin face and the dead eyes of a fish entered. He waited until the man came to him as if unwilling to let the foulness of the room touch him any further than necessary. After a whispered conversation, not in English, the man left and the one sitting gathered his notes and followed.

The interrogator studied her, showing actual interest for the first time. "Your partner was the one we wanted and he is, you will be sad to learn, he is dead. Our men killed him this morning." He shrugged. "You are free to go. I understand your embassy has sent a car."

Sensing a trick, she hesitated but he moved aside and she stood. Another guard held the door. Quickly, she walked across the room, half expecting a bullet in the back.

"Too bad, it would have been such fun to interrogate you further. Maybe we will meet again, who knows?"

She did not turn around.

#   #

Miles away, deep into the Czechia countryside outside a bustling village just south of Děčín not far from the German border on the Elbe river, a young woman not yet out of her teens, pretty more from her youth than real beauty stepped outside and smiled. Her light, almost blond hair was braided down her back and her worn winter coat, nearly outgrown, was open as the sun brought warmth after the night's chill. Maya Knezevic loved when spring arrived. Since a child she had loved being outdoors, running in the fields, someone always chasing her, "Don't go too far, Maya dear, you're too young."

She was no longer too young and was given the awesome responsibility of tending the goats. Their herd of goats was the mainstay for their small farm. Chickens gave eggs and one pig was slaughtered every year but the goats gave milk and cheese and butter. In the spring new baby goats appeared. She was told not to get attached, most were sold to neighboring farmers or given as wedding presents. She couldn't help herself and if she grew overly attached she would hide that one. She had hiding spots she hoped no one knew about.

The Knezevic clan was large, aunts and uncles and cousins all lived within a few miles of each other. Birthdays and holidays were large food filled affairs. Maya Knezevic, though, was restless. More was out there, she could feel it. She wasn't yet old enough to strike out on her own but an elderly neighbor to whom she took food let her borrow his books. Many days she would lay under a tree and read, trying to remember to keep one eye on her goats.

That day however, the sun on her face, she fell asleep reading *Anne of Green Gables*, another young girl who lived on a farm with relatives although she had no idea where Canada was let alone Prince Edward Island. She'd found an old map but didn't see anything called Canada on it.

When she woke with a start she knew immediately Petros was missing. He was her problem goat, she loved him dearly and he was not with the herd. She ran around looking for him, not calling too loudly because if anyone knew he didn't behave they would sell him.

Finally, she heard a faint bleat. Petros had slid down the muddy embankment and was exhausted trying to climb out. With melting snow the river was dangerous, she had to be very careful. Slowly, she made her way and grabbed Petros by the collar and dragged him back up. She looked around, grateful that no one had seen her. She shooed him back to the herd.

She realized her scarf, hand knitted by Auntie My after whom she was named, had caught on a tree branch. With trepidation she started down again. Just as she rescued her scarf she noticed something else. She peered closer, at the prone and lifeless body of a man. Lodged partially between a log and underbrush along the soft bank after the water receded, covered in mud, he was barely recognizable as a person.

Her expression was more confusion than fear, at an unusual sight in her simple world. She could see the goats, all of them, enjoying the smorgasbord of tasty eats after spring rains.

She continued to stare, unsure what to do. She'd seen dead bodies before; in hill country many people die, the old and infirm and the young in accidents. Yet she couldn't tell which state he was in. And even if he wasn't dead, she wasn't sure what to do. She took care of goats not people.

Her decision made she ran to her nearest neighbor who was her uncle or cousin, she was never entirely sure. She banged on the door, "Uncle Valtar, Uncle Valtar, you must come."

A large man with an explosion of gray hair answered the door. "*Zdravey*, hello little Maya, why do you yell so?"

She pointed back to the river. Valtar tossed away the napkin around his neck and followed her.

#   #

Two days later Valerie looked decidedly different from her previous interrogation. She had showered, been given new clothes and a long night of rest. Not sleep, still rattled by recent events, sleep hadn't come. As she looked about she had a sense of déjà vu, another interrogation room, this time with fresh pale green paint, full windows with open maroon curtains although a gray sky, comfortable chair and no obvious brute force. Again she sat waiting, expressionless but in a conference room in Munich.

That didn't make it any less perilous.

She studied the woman sitting across from her who continued to read from a file marked "Rhodes, Valerie." She had introduced herself as Melissa Gallagher, Assistant Deputy Director, C.I.A.. Nearly six feet in heels and rail thin, her hair was perfectly highlighted, complexion flawless possibly with the help of Botox; high maintenance, top to bottom. Not the usual civil servant blandness. Gallagher had aspirations. Public speaking did not seem to be one of them.

Debrief after an assignment was standard operating procedure; actually it was mandatory. What was not standard was a debrief by an A.D.D., more than a few pay grades above the usual team and meant the proceedings were need to know, as in fewer the better and that's too many. She had come to Munich specifically to debrief her. Not a good sign.

Yet so far the questions she had been asked were basic:

Why so long in the wind? *Train schedule, hid in a group tour.*

Who set the venue? *H.Q.*

Who changed the venue? *I don't know.*

How was it transmitted? *By text.*

Coded? *An older one.*

She paused at that.

How much time elapsed? *Two hours.*

How did they find your hideout? *I don't know.*

Why did you separate from your partner?

She had no intention of giving him up or admitting their hideout was compromised.

"He took the first watch."

The undercurrent was also different from S.O.P., not a surprise when everything had gone wrong. She had been captured and her partner, as far as she could tell, was missing. Her questions about him had been ignored. She wanted to pound it out of this women, she could take her easily but how many more waited just outside. She'd be locked away for assault and that would render her useless.

The only question Gallagher had answered was that she had arranged for her release from capture. She didn't explain how or why they had agreed to let her go but presumably it had to do with an exchange of some kind, money or prisoner. That answer was not her concern but she would sit here patiently until they deemed her fit to learn the whereabouts of her partner.

If he was…. no, she wasn't ready to face that and she had no intention of sharing anything else with this woman, no matter her lofty title.

To Valerie's surprise Gallagher smiled as she said. "You may call me Missy. Those who work for me do."

"In what capacity would that be?"

"I'm afraid your field operative days are over. This assignment went sour. Until we learn why and who was behind it, you're, how shall I put this, grounded. Whether you will be reassigned at a later date, I can't say. You will report to training."

She gathered her materials and stood to leave.

"Training for what?"

Missy smiled again, less sincerely. "Didn't I say? You've shown an aptitude for tracking money. Until now, it's only been part of your field work but I head up that unit and frankly, I welcome your skills as part of the team."

Like hell you say. Aloud, she said, "I want to know about my partner. I'm a field agent. I intend to stay a field agent. With my partner."

Missy frowned. "I'm afraid that's not possible. We have no information at this time. Until we do you are assigned to my unit. It's not negotiable. Of course you can resign but then you would be a private citizen, limited travel during the investigation and any contact completely unavailable to you. Your choice."

Valerie stared. She didn't trust herself to speak.

"Good. It's settled. See you in a week. The country thanks you for your service and more to come."

Valerie was seething. They were going to throw Joshua under the bus for their own failure and wanted her help to do it. And that was not going to happen, not as long as she was breathing. She'd be their good little soldier for as long as it took to find him.

Then she'd kill him herself, for abandoning her.

#   #

The sun began to set on a wood cabin, appearing small from the outside, but was in fact quite roomy on the inside. The large dining and living room was clearly the focus of everything family. A large wooden table dominated, likely assembled from the nearby forest, and would seat a dozen comfortably. A hallway in back led to bedrooms and storage. The kitchen was not modern, the stove that still cooked with wood dominated but with room for several to move about at once.

Next to a large rock fireplace with a robust fire, in an alcove, was a cot, covered with colorful blankets. A gathering of generations, by their looks all related, went about their business, another hard day's end when all are together cooking and laughing and talking. Each in turn cast furtive looks at the cot.

Finally, as dinner was being set to table, the blankets stirred amid a groan. Food forgotten, with much relief, all rushed to the bedside to see.

Joshua, sweating under the pile of blankets, opened his eyes, momentarily confused to see the concerned and curious expressions of the gathered Knezevic household who were staring down at him like archaeologists at a new species discovery. Noted were the scruffy beard and bandaged head with dried blood that had seeped out above his left eye. Someone insisted he have a few sips of water. He struggled to swallow and groaned in pain as he shifted his weight.

Collectively, he heard a gasp.

"He is awake."

"I can see that. I am right here."

"Who is he?"

"Yesterday we did not know. Today we do not know."

"Go get Maya, she will want to see the man she saved."

"He should have soup."

"We will ask him if he wants soup."

"Everyone wants soup."

"Then bring him soup."

"Saved?" Joshua said, his voice croaking. "Where am I?"

"You are here, of course. But we will wait, Maya will get to tell you. She brought you in from the river. You were dead."

"Quick, bring him some strong tea with lots of honey."

"He wasn't dead. See? If he's not dead now he wasn't dead yesterday."

"Yes, saved, you were found on the riverbank by our Maya. You were nearly frozen to death but we had men here to carry you and a big fire."

"And soup. I always have soup."

"Yes, Mama, and good soup it is."

"Where am I?"

"Right here, we watch over you, at turns. I am Valtar, this is Johan, over there is…."

But Joshua had passed out again.

"Never mind the soup."

A week later, skies clear, Mama's soup having done it's restorative power, Joshua was clean shaven with only a small bandage a sign of his injury. Still weak, he walked slowly with Maya in the field, kaleidoscopic with bloom.

"I like when the cold is gone and the rain leaves flowers. I can put them in my hair and pretend I'm at a dance."

"Have you ever been to a dance?"

"No. I am too young. But sometimes I get to watch. And I practice, so I'll be ready."

"You'll be the belle of the ball."

"Bell? Like on my goats?"

"No, Belle is also a French word that means a very pretty woman. That's what you will be when you grow up."

"Really? You think so?"

"I know so." He walked ahead, he needed to think.

She caught up. "You are troubled. Like my goats, they do not eat, they are not well."

He smiled. "You're very perceptive."

"What does that mean, persi.. per…"

"Perceptive. It means smart."

"Then why do you not say smart?"

"You're right, of course. You're very smart. I'm troubled because my friend is lost. I cannot find her."

"Did you put a bell around her neck? Not the French one, though. I put a bell around the neck of my goats then they do not get lost."

He smiled. "I did not think of that. I will do that next time."

She ran off to tend her goats. He walked to a nearby tree to stare out over the terrain. "Where are you, Vally?" He turned to head back in, time to go, head wound or not he had to find her and quickly. He'd rattle every contact until she was found. If she was still….

He refused to go there. Suddenly, just as he turned toward the house his mind flashed backward, years, when his mother was dying. A small boy, at her bedside, crying. His mother, her face pale, a nurse hovering, another man trying to comfort him but he was unconsolable. The adults glanced at each other, it was only a matter of time.

Unsteady, he reached to grab the tree, breathing hard. The vision overtook him, how he'd been pulled away, screaming, when strangers arrived. His father had stood above him, stoic but firm, as he'd told the boy to go to his room, he'd be up later.

Obedient, he went but he'd broken free to watch from the top of the staircase. No one would tell him where they were taking his mother, she wasn't moving; he'd understood only that his world had forever changed.

By the time his father had appeared, a long time after, Joshua would only stare at the wall, mute. If his father had said anything comforting he had not heard.

Nearly an hour later, Maya returned. He was on the ground, his eyes fixated ahead. She reached out to touch him, unsure what to do.

He reacted abruptly, grabbed her by the arm, ready to twist, when he realized what he'd almost done. He let go and she jumped back, afraid.

"I'm sorry, I didn't mean to hurt you."

"Mr. Joshua. Are you okay? You do not look okay."

"I was having a bad dream."

"I can call my uncle to get you. He said I should tell you there are men in the village asking about you. He only listened but knew they would find out. He says there are no secrets in such a small town. Is that true?"

He knew the risk the family took by harboring him so long. He smiled at her. "You're a very good girl and also smart. Thank you for telling me this. Because you did, I have a very great favor to ask of you. Can you keep a secret?"

She frowns. "I don't know. I only have one secret. I found a book one day, in another language, and I didn't tell anyone. I hid it so that one day I can travel to that country."

"Then I will keep that secret for you. The men who search for me, they will want you to tell them where I went. I don't want them to find me."

Solemnly, she nodded. "I will tell no one, not even my uncles. You are my friend now."

"Yes, Maya, I am your friend now and you are my friend." He held out his hand and she placed her small hand in his.

She smiled. Two secrets. She was rich, indeed.

#   #

Being off the grid wasn't unusual in his line of work but if he checked in now, after a botched assignment, he'd be recalled. They would mine him for all the

48

mission information, his partner left behind, generating a report to cover asses. He had no idea how they were discovered shortly after a venue change but luck had nothing to do with it. Someone had set them up and he would find Valerie and then find out who and why.

The quickest way to find her was to stay off the grid. For that he needed money but couldn't use the sanctioned account numbers made available to field agents, that would red flag his location.

Like most agents he kept an account in reserve but he needed more, fast, and that meant a collect call to an exchange memorized even as he swore he'd never use it.

The phone was answered after a few prompts of verification. He made arrangements to pick up funds the next day then braced himself as he was forwarded to another exchange, to explain what else he needed.

Finding Vally was more important than his pride.

# #

Ivan Kominsky was tired. He was always tired. Life on a farm was tiring. Pigs needed slop, cows needed milking, vegetables needed tending from rabbits and pests, horses needed hay, every day sunup to sundown something needed doing. Repairs, roofs leaked, animals died, it never ended. What he would give to make it all go away. He'd tried, he'd gone to the city but jobs were scarce. After a year doing pickup work for a series of cheating overlords and no money to better himself he returned, the stench of failure more pronounced than that from the pigs.

His father, Sergey Kominsky, however, was delighted at the return of his only son. His four daughters had married, two moved away and the other two busy with babies and their husbands. His wife and Ivan's mother had died long ago, farm life leaving her few options. For a while it was the two of them. They worked side by side as Ivan gradually realized this was his life. Maybe he would find a woman to marry him but in this isolated part of the world so near the Slovakian border and with brutal winters, pickings were slim. A widow or two, maybe, with brats of their own, not even pretending to love him but wanting a meal ticket. He might have succumbed but he knew they would never accept the rough life of farmer's wife. It would be like having one more cow to milk but without the butter.

At night he and his father had sat around the fireplace smoking their pipes, while his father reminisced about the old days. He had been a resister in the revolutions, there seemed to be many or maybe his memory crisscrossed into different decades. It didn't matter, they were good stories and he could imagine his father a hero, with contacts around the world, even in America.

America. How he would like to live there where everyone was rich, certainly richer than here. He knew they had farms too, he'd read up a little, a big swath in the middle that didn't have so many people so they must grow the food. Would it be better, farming in America? Probably not. And so he had spent his nights listening to his father's stories of the old days when he worked against repression. Occasionally Ivan had wondered how much was true and how much was an old man's pretense but as they sat as equals, companions, he didn't think it mattered. Those days were long gone. Life wasn't what one could call good but it wasn't as harsh as back then, when life and livelihoods had dangled precariously. And they ate well.

Ivan was stout. All muscle after his years working the farm but he was not a good looking man by anyone's judgement. His thick hair was thinning, his beard was dark making him look menacing unless he shaved but lately why bother, who would notice? He thought he was a good man, his father had often told him that. He tried to stay clean, taking soap to the river once a week maybe less when frozen. He made do. That's what he thought of himself, a good man who made do.

One day his father didn't wake up. The neighbor pronounced him dead, no doubt his heart. He had called in the proper authorities to record it, the farm was already in his name and so he continued, day after lonely day. What else could he do?

That morning, as Ivan headed for the barn and the restless cows, he saw high above the stables a tall stranger leaning against a tree and watching him. He was quite still, looking a little weary.

Predators were a source of worry to his chickens and he kept his eyes on alert for anything unusual. A stranger was not unheard of; hikers and lost tourists occasionally wandered through, wanting water and directions. He offered no more, he was not a diner although sometimes he thought maybe he could charge but too few came to be worth the bother this far inland. He continued in the barn and his chores, only slightly curious, a new thought to counter the drudgery. When he looked again, the stranger was gone. Good riddance, he thought.

Joshua, on the ridge, had spent no little time finding the Kominsky farm. He couldn't just wander around asking; he wasn't sure who was looking for him, or why. He hoped Sergey Kominsky still had contacts and could help him. His father had once told him that in this part of the world Sergey was a friend. He had done much to save allies, at great risk to himself. He was probably an old man and the person down there was not old. Probably his son or a farmhand. Now that he'd found the farm he needed to be sure it still belonged to Sergey. He moved out of sight and waited, to see how many people lived here. Satisfied it was just the one he found a secure place to rest until dark. He was getting old, injuries took longer to heal and his body ached from the travel, from having to avoid main arteries and being observed.

Just before dark Ivan finished up the second milking, his final chore, and headed for the house with his milk jug. He'd not seen the man again as he fed chickens and pigs, put horses in the pasture, tightened a fence post and so forgot about him.

At the door, without warning someone grabbed him. He started to resist and was put in a throat lock, unable to move.

"What do you want? I have no money." He tried to keep fear out of his voice.

"Open the door and go inside."

"No, you can't...." The arm tightened. How was it possible this skinny person could be so strong. But he did as he was told, setting the milk container on the shelf.

Inside, the man lessened his hold as he said, "Where's Sergey Kominsky?"

Too surprised to lie, Ivan answered, "He's dead. Two years ago. I am his son. This is my farm and you are trespassing." He tried to sound firm but the man ignored him.

"What's your name?"

"Ivan."

"What's for dinner? I'm hungry and I've come a long way to see your father."

Ivan stared.

"I can pay for it."

"I was going to heat up a stew. It's only me..." he wondered if he should admit to being alone, if this was a robbery.

"That's fine. Is there enough?"

"Yes. I cook large batches at once."

"Good. Then we can talk."

Ivan, now more curious than afraid set about to start the fire in the stove and told the stranger to make one in the fireplace. He pulled out the stew from the porch where it stayed cold. He added a loaf of bread that didn't look stale and some fresh butter. He poured two large glasses of milk. When the stranger looked oddly at that, he said, slightly defensive.

"I have cows. They give milk. I sell some in the village, with eggs from the chickens. I keep some. If you don't want..."

"No, it's fine, thank you."

"Who are you?"

"My name is Joshua Daine. Your father knew my father."

Ivan was shocked. So his father's stories were true. He had never missed his father like he did at that moment. He knew the name of course and his father had often bragged about his "friend" from America. But could he trust this man? And more important, how much would he pay?

"What is it you want?"

"Information. I was hoping he still had some contacts."

Ivan hesitated. "Why should I help you? I am a peaceful man. My father's business, that was a long time ago."

"It's important."

This Joshua Daine was being friendly but something in his voice said it would not be wise to argue. And the strength he had used around his neck was memorable. Ivan didn't see a weapon and wondered if maybe he didn't need one to kill.

"He might have told me some things. I cannot promise. What is it you want to know?"

The next morning Ivan went into the village with his milk and eggs. The old men at the store were always willing to talk. Usually he had no time for them but today he would listen and get the information for Mister Daine, just like his father had done. For a price of course, just like his father.

In Ivan Komisky's life this was his best day ever.

It might have been Ivan Kominsky's best day, to feel a hero like his father but he wasn't his father. Sergey had grown up under repressive regimes, he'd watched his father gunned down for resisting soldiers trying to rape his sister. From then on his family lived in fear.

For survival Sergey had learned to hunt rabbit at night and steal to feed his family. His sister had never recovered, always fearful and delicate, his mother angry and harsh. Eventually Sergey joined with a neighbor to work against the new regime. Ivan was born long after and never learned stealth.

And so it was. Ivan Kominsky's questions at the gathering place of old men was unusual and to old men whose days never change, it was notable. Notable events get shared. Men who knew of his father but had not participated had instead kept their distance for their own protection. They lived in silence to quell their fear. When Ivan began asking questions about a missing woman they were curious and curious old men talk among themselves.

One of the old men had left for a while, to speak to his brother-in-law who was well connected. He had learned that yes, a woman had been held at the *Ceska* cells but had left. Her people had traded a lot of money for her, he thought. Maybe it was her. Maybe not.

And so Ivan, armed with information about the woman, feeling proud of his accomplishment and future income source that he hadn't noticed he was being followed.

Joshua, knowing Ivan was not up to the mission but intent on learning of Valerie's whereabouts was well prepared and saw them coming from his hilltop perch.

Ivan was disappointed to find his benefactor gone but as money was left on the table he decided maybe being a spy was not for him, worlds change. He would use the money to fix up the farm to sell it and start a new life. But even as he fixed his cold stew again he knew he would not.

He turned when he heard a noise from the hall, thinking it was Daine. It was not, as he stared at the barrel of a rifle.

"Sit. Where is the man who wants this information?" Ivan sat, ruing the moment he saw the stranger.

"I don't know. He was here when I left."

"We will wait. He will not leave without his information."

After dark, Joshua entered silently through the back door. In the dim light he saw the gun to Ivan's head and two others, armed.

"Gentlemen," said Joshua, in Polish, not his best language but he'd get by. "Good of you to stop by. Ivan, why don't you make these gentlemen some tea?"

One of the guards waved his gun. "We're not here to drink tea. You will come with us."

Joshua smiled. "I can make you a much better offer. One that includes money, that no one will know about. A lot of money."

He had their attention. "You see, all I want is information, nothing more, and I can pay for it." He stopped smiling, his voice icy. "But if you lie to me, make something up, I'll kill you and your families."

"We have the guns. You are our prisoner."

At lightning speed, before they can think to move, Joshua had grabbed the one foolish enough to stand too close thinking a gun was a deterrent to this stranger, taken his gun and used him as a shield. The others were too stunned to react and unsure whether to shoot or surrender.

"Of course you may shoot and you'll both be dead, along with your friend if your aim is good. Or you can give your guns to him while we discuss your fees."

Ivan jumped up, nearly knocking over his chair and grabbed the two guns. He placed them on the counter where he stayed hoping to avoid whatever trouble might appear but excited all the same. Soon the rag tag soldiers left, with guns empty of bullets to Ivan's relief.

For the next few days Joshua helped Ivan around the farm. He'd never worked around animals, there were horses at boarding school, for the competitions, but well cared for by others. He had weeded a few herb gardens as punishment for infractions but the smell of pigs was unique. Milking a cow was not so easy. You'd think getting milked twice a day would teach them better manners, he grumbled as Ivan laughed, happy to have someone to whom he could show off his skills. Maybe he'd make improvements after all with some of the money and find a woman to marry. Watching Joshua cut logs to stack for the winter fires and gather eggs he realized how desperate he was for companionship.

Three days later two of the guards returned. They placed a pile of newspapers on the table, pointed to a headline that said there was turmoil in the Middle East. So? Always turmoil there. They'd heard more, that it was being set up by American interests that wanted war. Guns to sell, oil to purchase, raising prices, always profits, you Americans.

The other one nudged him, don't insult this man. He whined that so much subterfuge was not easy to obtain without suspicion and they should be paid more. Joshua did not argue but before handing it over made it clear that Ivan knew nothing, that his continued health was very important and keeping quiet about their transaction equally important. Things had a way of backfiring on the messenger, keep that in mind.

The two nodded solemnly, took their money and left, happy to be rid of that madman.

Joshua shook hands with Ivan, left him enough money to hire someone and headed out.

What he didn't know was why Valerie had been set up. Maybe someone had intercepted a message but her phone was coded, someone would need to know specifically her phone and how to decipher. Was she used as bait for something else or was the computer stick used as bait for her? Was she a sacrifice to get the information? He checked his pants pocket, still there and hopefully still readable.

He had to know what was on it. Maybe it would tell him who had put a hit on his partner; she might be safe for now but until he knew who and why he didn't know for how long.

In the military his squad would play a drinking game, who would you kill in cold blood if it served a higher purpose? He'd thought it a harmless macho release and rarely took part but now he had his answer.

\#   \#

Chapter 4

Inside a large open room in a nondescript building surrounded by other nondescript government buildings sat Valerie Rhodes, seated between a young bespectacled man who occasionally glanced her way and a woman who had eyes on the clock. Each diligently worked in their government issued cubicles, checking a series of numbers on the government issued computer screens in front of them. All wore neck lanyards with photo I.D.s.

Her hair was shorter, cut in a simple chin length and her pale striped blue shirt one of a dozen or so picked up when reassigned to fit a dress code of the professional woman not aiming for the executive suite. On her feet, however, were athletic shoes, having come up short in the stylish shoe department. She saw no reason to change shoes from street to office just to sit in a chair. No one mentioned it and most assumed it to be her little rebellion like Joseph's colorful socks or Debbie's blue fingernails. The room was filled with identical cubicles but silent, each person scanning their screens with equal intensity. Occasionally, someone would pause, then head into the back office with a report. That might result in further Instructions to all or added to the daily top secret memo with updated information.

Behind the open space work area was a large office, expensively furnished in a non-standard government issue style and empty, not just of a person but of anything personal. No photos or plaques or even magazines. Old Ironpants as he was known, not always affectionately by his team, which they believed he was unaware of but he was, in fact, totally aware of almost everything that went on not just by his staff but around the world. He had long cultivated a bit of a doofus reputation, more interested in his golf handicap and aged Scotch but was quite the opposite. It served him well. His first lesson in spy craft was always let them underestimate you. Always let them think you're nobody; it's far more effective in gathering information not to mention staying alive. Surprise was your friend. He taught that to all new recruits, few used it as effectively.

The only other office facing the room was inhabited by Melissa Gallagher, pacing as she often did, dressed as if born to the executive suite. Her focus was absolute when it came to eliminating any barrier to replace Monroe Oliver Kellenstone III, the missing occupant of the neighboring office, to become Deputy Director of the C.I.A. He'd sent her to Munich for God knows why to interview that pathetic field agent then demanded, in that obsequious way she loathed, that she be brought into her unit. Still irritated by orders without context, not unusual but she was his number two with highest clearance and a future, not some secretary who might blab. Nonetheless, checking her work over the past few months she had to admit Rhodes was an asset. Just not her asset.

Gallagher smiled only when it served a purpose other than pleasantries. Knowing this and knowing that leadership required some sense of familiarity she introduced herself with, "Call me Missy, and my door is always open." She hated her stupid childhood nickname, given to her by parents thinking it was cute that a toddler couldn't pronounce three syllables. She had put way too much work into climbing this ladder and she wasn't going to slip over a name. Her staff soon realized the open door was more a literal policy than preferred.

The wall clock eased past 7 p.m. and banks were long closed over the continent followed by Caribbean hours for "special" customers. By ones and twos the room emptied, a few cited weekend plans. One person looked back as if to say, "day's over, Val" but decided against it. Valerie rarely ate with them or showed up to after work drinks parties. They all knew she'd been a field agent amid rumors circulated that something had gone wrong and she was being punished with a desk assignment. But for a group of computer geeks tracking illegal money all over the globe they knew better than try to hack her records. Anyone caught accessing unauthorized C.I.A. files would not just be out of a job but could be charged under the Official Secrets Act and that only a fool would mess with. And certainly not to be the first with office gossip.

Geeks were a different breed, they knew computers. Field agents, though, knew the players. Each group was a little bit in awe of the other although all but Valerie managed basic office protocol of social interaction. Whatever secrets she held would not be sussed out by anyone there.

Missy sat at her desk, restless, moved a pencil around, checked her phone, opened her computer, closed it again. A woman on the move was not patient. Her recent trip to Munich was ostensibly to coordinate with the *Politzei* over terrorist threats, as such she'd had to attend a couple of meetings. She'd met someone. The relationship was new and that made her vulnerable and Missy hated feeling vulnerable. Almost as much as she hated waiting for a phone call. She'd had many relationships fall away as her career absorbed her and she accepted that. This was different, she felt or was led to believe that this one might help not hurt her career.

Growing up she'd been lonely, an only child in a military family, moving often, father deployed. Not a bad childhood but her father had rank and they'd lived off base. As military her school mates didn't understand. Most had two parents even if separated or a step parent and siblings. Noise at dinner, that's what she'd always equated with happy families. Yet here she was, usually working past the dinner hour, a few business events, a few dates that usually went nowhere.

She had just decided to call it day when her phone buzzed. She waited for two rings to pick it up.

"Gallagher." Her expression softened, relieved, as she swiveled to face the wall. "Hi, I'm glad you called. I'm finished now, are you in town?" She listened, her expression registering disappointment. "Yes, I understand, of course, that comes first. No, I'm fine, I just miss..." She laughed softly. "What? Yes, she's still here. Why do you.... right, soon, yes, we'll...."

The caller gave her no chance to finish or say goodbye. Missy hung up, grabbed her purse and coat, headed out.

"Going to be here long, Val? They're shutting down the heat, checking vents again."

Valerie looked up, loathing the phony bonhomie from her supervisor.

"Just running through some final numbers."

"Anything interesting?"

"I thought so for a minute but seems not. Earlier deposits we've already traced. I'll start again Monday, see if any movement."

"Good, keep me posted. Have a good weekend." She left without waiting for an answer.

At 7:45 p.m. Valerie finally stood up, sure that everyone had left and she wouldn't have to make small talk. She stretched and pulled her purse out of a locked drawer and went to the closet for her coat. Outside, in the secure parking lot she went to her late model Toyota and key carded out. She didn't notice someone in the shadows watching her. Even if she had it was a building of spooks; someone was always watching someone.

#   #

Another nondescript office, but furnished in bland and soothing colors like psychiatrist offices everywhere. It could be anywhere but it wasn't anywhere, it was deep in a secret government building in Virginia, not far from Langley, C.I.A. headquarters. It was as secure and as secret as any building in Washington could be.

Dr. Linda Cheng, PhD, was their top interrogator and their top debrief analyst. Her wall was covered with awards and diplomas, a woman who could have earned a lot more money in the private sector but felt a call to duty. She'd worked for a while as a prosecuting attorney but found it unsatisfying, more about plea bargains than justice and rarely just. The law had many mistresses and all were demanding. When an opening came for the C.I.A., as a trainer, she believed she could put her knowledge to use in a way that would have more impact. It was a perfect fit. Her control issues satisfied by her innovative methods she turned out top agents well prepared to serve their country. Much espionage was being done by computer, scouring the Internet and dark net for secrets; no one it seems, wanted to stay quiet. Thinking the Internet anonymous they couldn't resist a brag or two. Tracking money often located terrorist cells. No one could operate without funding. No democratic government could operate without laws. She would teach that so much fell apart when an agent broke a law or posted anything unsanctioned.

She had also trained a top notch team of undercover agents and became highly effective at getting post assignment debrief information from the most recalcitrant of subjects. One of whom, Joshua Daine, was in front of her now. Neither was happy with the other. One man whose own Internet presence, she was sure, was nonexistent. Ironically his cover as his father's son did have coverage and even though useful in his work she was sure he'd erase it if he could.

No small part of her success was based on her disarming looks, barely over five feet although she wore heels as a matter of pride and colorful silk dresses, often with a color coordinated tailored jacket. Her pearls were genuine and her dark hair seriously maintained. To the casual observer she had the outward appearance of a valued trophy wife. It wasn't far from her reality. While she was married to a professor of International Relations at George Washington University and while she attended numerous faculty events with a supportive smile, in truth it was a marriage of convenience as both preferred same sex relationships. They had been childhood friends in Nashville where Asian families were few and it was understood by all they would fall in love and marry. Early on they had realized it was their best option. Both excelled at university and she, by virtue of her ability to read people and disarm them, studied medicine and psychiatry at G.W. and then excelled at Georgetown Law. If she ever stopped to think about it she'd realize she had a very good life. But she never looked backward; it was her gift to her success, waste no time on what can't be changed.

Yet apparently that was exactly what she was doing. Joshua Daine was not in post traumatic stress from time spent in a Russian gulag, as the file stated, nor had he gone off the grid amid worries that he had sold out, the actual reason for his mandatory visits. Of that she was sure. She knew something had gone very wrong but that was the risk of the job and he was trained for it. He also had a well connected father and even the Russians, if he were anywhere near them which she doubted, were careful whom they beat up beyond recognition.

He was in remarkable shape for having been locked up. She had wondered about that and requested his file to see if he'd been given special treatment but it had minimal information. She had the highest clearance and would have seen all of it had it been available.

No, work related injuries weren't his problem. Whatever it was went deeper, way down. The file she was given said he was bitter by having such a high profile father and still being dumped in a gulag, it had hit a nerve. But her attempts to get him to even mention his father had been met with stony silence or once telling her to "read Forbes Magazine if you're interested."

She notated his silence but did not dispute the prepared information. Not yet. Not until she knew why one was at odds with the other. Daily she checked her office for listening devices, on her own as she'd learned to trust no one. It would also be useful information to have if something appeared before a particular appointment.

He dressed well for these occasions. Today in dark brown slacks, black silk shirt. She'd heard her secretary gasp when he'd first appeared and always managed to be at her desk when he arrived. He had a reputation as a playboy - did they still call it that? Relationships that didn't last, always on the move. That alone would keep her busy in a normal session.

"You've been off the grid for a while. That makes people in your field very nervous. They wonder what you might have been up to or who you might be working for. Your father arranged for you to be part of a prisoner exchange but I think we both know you were no where near a Russian prison. It's a good cover, avoids those pesky questions. Now my job is to debrief you to see if you've been turned. I'd stake my reputation that no one can turn you. So that's one box checked."

She gave him a minute to absorb how much she knew about him but she needed more and wasn't sure how long they would let her keep him. So far he'd been quite agreeable to keeping his appointments but not so interested in participating.

"What's it like to have a father that can pull such strings?"

She was trying to push his button but he wasn't having it. He'd been ordered to see her daily for a month but she'd requested three times per week because staring at each other was a waste of her time. Once they actually read. She thought if she provided no interest, going through the motions, it would open him up. It didn't.

"You know I have the power to return you to work or not. You had a head wound. They're tricky, sometimes open doors we'd rather keep shut." He didn't move, continued to watch her hanging fern over the window. She had to use a ladder to water it but she treated it like the child she never thought of having. He was tall enough to easily do that for her and she had no doubt he would but also an infringement on her space.

"You are of course heir to a fortune so I suppose losing your job isn't something on your front burner." At that he glanced over. She knew that would spark interest, she'd just hoped for an actual reaction.

"In all this time you've never once asked about your partner." And at that, she was the recipient of a stare so dark she almost shivered. Now I've met the legendary Joshua Daine, she told herself, finally able to check off the mental box that told her she'd found her way in. But she knew better than to pursue it now, it would be useful again.

"One of these days, Joshua, you'll realize that talking to someone can be very helpful. I'm not your friend but find someone you can trust. What you tell me is confidential only as it doesn't pertain to the health of your ability to do your job. But a friend, a bartender, a fortune teller, a bum on the beach, someone. I mean it, before it does a deeper dive and you can't get out. I know something happened, you know it too and you need to manage it."

When she'd finished he stood up, knowing the hour was up without looking at his watch. He moved for the door when her phone rang. She frowned, her assistant knew there were no interruptions during sessions although she also knew it was over.

"Yes?" She listened. "Joshua, please wait a minute." He turned. She listened another minute, said thank you and hung up.

"I hope you appreciate the irony. A therapy session trying to find out the dynamic of your relationship to your father and he has summoned you. He says it's important and will expect you for dinner. I trust you know the way."

"Why would I be surprised? He's the reason I'm here." He left, quietly shutting the door.

#   #

Chapter 5

Bennett Daine's large estate, called simply Daine House, was tucked away outside the Washington, D.C. suburbs in the hills of Virginia, far back from any public road. Nothing could be seen by the occasional passing traffic or even a news helicopter looking for a scoop as to the latest cabinet member sighting. He ran in the best circles, a top donor, but few suspected his reach was far deeper than money. The most influential people in the universe were a scrambled phone call away, most on a first name basis. He could influence votes although he rarely tried. America was his adopted country and he would never interfere in her most basic tenant. He was a true patriot in the old fashioned sense of the word. America had brought him wealth and privilege and he felt that obligation keenly; only in America could he have amassed his fortune legally. He had a head for figures and back before stocks were traded on computers and currency trades were done by hand he could do it faster and better, in his head. He was held in awe by those in his company.

Then one day, tired of wheeling and dealing and new technology he sold out and retired to the estate he rarely saw. Or so he told everyone. In truth, he began to court his clients not for their money but for their influence. He had built a solid reputation and networking skills so that his success translated into an entirely new arena.

Bennett Daine did not understand failure. He had eliminated it from his life and his surroundings, quickly and permanently. His persona was public knowledge, at least the background he'd created for himself was well known, all except the one secret he had told no one. Only Yevgeny Yurovinsky knew of it and was a participant in it but each man trusted the other to never reveal it. It was the strength of their friendship. And that made him instantly agree to protect Lina Yurovinskova when he would have preferred to bring her swiftly to America. But if Yevi said she would be in Sweden then in Sweden he would protect her.

The weeks he'd endured waiting for word of Joshua had nearly done him in. Loss he would learn to handle but not knowing was worse than he'd ever imagined. Lately he began to feel his tough exterior was a façade. Enough contacts remained that he could easily have arranged for his son's return unharmed from an eastern bloc prison. Some said that's where he was. A few hesitantly said word was he'd been killed. Most had heard nothing. He never gave up, he would find him no matter how long.

Then one day out of the blue his son had contacted him. Relief washed over him like a spring waterfall then anger at the long days while he'd tried to get word. He wanted to ask what happened, how was he, when was he coming home, so desperate was he for information.

Joshua gave away nothing. All he got was a terse, "Later, now I need you to spread word you're negotiating my release, you have it in hand and call them off looking. Replenish the account, I don't know yet what I'll need."

Bail him out? That was the last thing his son would want from him after a lifetime of resisting everything he owned and wanted for him. But hearing his voice and the pure joy of that infused him so that he'd instantly agreed.

Unsure of why his son resented him for his success he nonetheless knew he did. Because he was self made he had only wanted to teach him the value of duty and honor. The loss of his wife and Joshua's mother, he knew, was an insurmountable blow to them both. But time for grieving was past; his son had apparently not yet learned that lesson. Well, it was time. They had only each other. The Daine estate would one day belong to him; both were aware of that but only one seemed aware of that obligation.

Joshua had made it clear he wanted nothing to do with him or his money, even when he had needed it and that irritated Bennett. His son was stubborn, inherited from his father if he were honest.

Now though he had to step up, for Yevi, for Bennett's past, his too if it came to that. Joshua was the only one he trusted with this mission, not just to succeed but off the books. The forum would be watched and their presence would be as family friend. They'd sit together, guests of the keynote speaker. A reception was planned for after, they would socialize and Joshua would get Lina alone, a romantic interlude, explain the plan. She would agree, Yevi had said coming to America was her dream. He had tried over the years to bring her to England but something always interfered.

She was married to a highly placed man in the government and was afraid they would hunt her, kill them both, especially after recent poisonings of defectors.

Joshua would not refuse, not now, as he usually did with suggestions from his father. He knew his father's relationship with Yevi and had spent time with Lina. He would succeed because of his legendary skill. How Bennett had learned to hate that, every assignment could be his last. But any attempt to pull him back was met with stronger resistance.

Not this time. After Lina was safe he'd insist although he wasn't entirely sure how effective it would be. He'd find a way. He would face his son honestly and trust him to see that duty to family always came first, whether one liked it or not.

A few miles away a late model BMW expertly swerved through early evening traffic on the two lane highway, slowed to turn onto a quiet country road with enough curves that speeding was dangerous. Joshua, at the wheel, seemed in no hurry and kept below the posted 40 m.p.h. Another five miles before he stopped in front of a shrubbery covered entrance and a barely visible guard post. He rolled down the window to verify his presence before he drove through and, knowing a call would announce his arrival, he took his time. It was after all a beautiful piece of land to be enjoyed.

Truthfully though he was nervous, not a normal emotion for him and one he disliked as showing weakness. He'd spent a lifetime not showing his real thoughts and had no intention of letting his father know how much he loathed a command performance to this new family homestead. It was never his home, bought long after he'd disappeared into the world of secrets and espionage. In fact, he'd only been here twice when his father was away. He would have preferred facing a firing squad to dinner alone with this man he barely knew and more to the point, disliked. He'd made his own way in the world and refused to give credit for his success to being Bennett Daine's son and heir. His need for his father's interference to cover the time he'd been off the grid locating his partner infuriated him. He did not appreciate the irony.

He knew his father checked on him from time to time and that also irritated him, that he was able to do that but he was wise enough to not do it directly and risk being told to stop. That he would not do and if he promised he would break it. The only thing Joshua understood about his father was that he never lied unless he wanted something. To his son that was an easy tell.

The large estate home finally came into view. It was a common style in the English countryside and occasionally copied more in the Hampton's than around here. His father had grown up in England, that much he knew about him but had married an American and moved to the States for her or more likely not being high born with limited options for his career.

He parked off to the side, no other cars were visible but a road leading around the side led to an eight car garage, housed with a black Mercedes sedan and Chevy Suburban for his father and various other household cars, as needed. Behind that was a field for helicopter landings. No security was visible but he knew

73

it was there and that they knew he knew it. He'd deal with that later.

He sat a minute, thinking. His being summoned was not a total surprise. He knew he owed his father an explanation so he would hear the man out. He wondered briefly if his father was seriously ill and how he would feel about that.

Suddenly he began to shake. He gripped the steering wheel and pulled in gulps of air. The last time he'd had dinner alone with his father was after his first year at Oxford at The Quad, part of The Old Bank on High Street, a refurbished cozy luxury hotel where his father always stayed when visiting his alma mater for the many alumni events. As a student he could never afford to eat there; as Bennett Daine he took pride in taking his son. That time he had reserved the back room, normally the library, for this private meeting.

It had not gone well. His father was still expecting his son to join his company and his son, unable to explain why he had no intention of doing that, instead blurted out he was joining the military. His father had been nonplussed and the son left mistaking confusion for disappointment. It was years before they would speak again.

Still shaky but under control, Joshua stepped out of his car and stood a moment, taking in a few more gulps of air, as he watched the house. He had dressed for the occasion, dark Brioni slacks and a pale blue cashmere sweater with a short dress wool coat in navy. Years ago, right before he left for Uni, as the British called it, when everything he did seemed to be wrong in his father's eyes, a lecture on appearances. But that was not a fight to have now.

His father would check him out, to see if he could read his mood and how the meeting would go. He knew he wasn't here for a fireside chat. Joshua had often felt he had been trained to work for the C.I.A. since infancy. His father, believing he owed his entire world to his adopted country, was willing to sacrifice his son at its altar. As a teenager his resentment ran hot but over the years their isolation grew until their few meetings became a parry and thrust affair. Both men, trained in the art of deception for business purposes also used it to derail their feelings from each other.

He headed for the door that, unsurprisingly, opened as he put his foot on the step.

"Master Joshua, it's good to see you." The elderly butler, who had watched over him since childhood when his father hadn't, allowed himself one tiny smile of recognition in his otherwise stiff perfection of the English butler he had trained to be.

"Uncle Gerry." His childhood nickname for Gerard. Whatever else was wrong in his life, Uncle Gerry was there for him. Of that he was sure.

"Your father is in the library. Dinner in an hour."

Neutral territory. No office filled with awards and photos with the famous and the infamous. No reminder that this was the great Bennett Daine, widower, one son. His wife had died of cancer, devastating a man who felt he could buy his way out of anything when the boy was ten; both were grief stricken and unable to communicate. This led to Bennett thinking boarding school would be better for him as he'd begun acting out.

It had the desired result, he behaved himself or at least didn't get caught in enough escapades that they wanted to lose Daine money or cachet. But father and son lost whatever closeness they might have gained by their shared loss.

This had led Bennett to eventually allow another woman in his life, to act as consort. Cortina D'Angelo had three daughters of eligible age and preferred to live in New York. He was fond of them and their mother but frankly too busy to think much about except when needed to enhance his image at an event. She kept up her end of the bargain with grace and charm. His son avoided all contact with them.

Bennett was pretending to read titles on a bookshelf when Joshua entered. Father and son stared at each other, unsure of how to begin. Finally, Bennett walked over and held out his hand. Hoping not to show his reluctance, at least yet, Joshua shook it.

"Thank you for coming."

"Did I have a choice?"

"You always have a choice." He tried not to make it sound like a gauntlet. "Would you like something to drink?"

Silence.

"How have you been?"

"Dispense with the pleasantries, you've no doubt been informed since your efforts were the official version. Thank you for that, by the way."

"Pleasantries? Weeks without knowing if you were alive or dead? You owe me an explanation."

"I was busy. Isn't that the standard Daine line?"

"Now you're not. You're here."

"I wanted to be there. I needed information. I needed you to call off the dogs. I had work to do."

"No one at the company knew where you were, off the reservation, so to speak. You finally return, they're ready to lock you up, interrogation not debrief. You know how that goes, months before you see light of day. If you hadn't called so I could put in motion your cover story, a ridiculous one at that but I suppose it was in everyone's interest to buy into it. What did you do that made them think you'd done a bunk? I had to offer assurances you were completing an assignment for me and someone got the wrong idea."

"A Daine negotiation with the C.I.A.. Who? Kellenstone, Old Ironpants?" He named the Deputy Director of the C.I.A. and a longtime ally. "Two titans doing what they do best, talk something to death. I'm sorry I missed it. How is he, by the way? Still in the driver's seat? I hear the new Administration doesn't take kindly to his straight as an arrow."

"When are you going to…. never mind that now. He's fine, so far, and you're right, the new administration is upending everything and not in a good way. Sit down. I have a favor to ask."

Joshua knew that much or he would not have called. Also why he felt he could push his behavior. How far his father let him go usually told him how badly he wanted what he was about to ask. Clearly, this was important.

He sat on the same brown leather chair where he'd received his first lecture on how to be a Daine, at age twelve. The next year he was off to boarding school and saw his father on occasional holidays. It was not a bonding experience. Their few attempts as adults often ended badly as by then each spoke a language of differing expectations.

"It's not for me. It's Yevi. He's giving a speech in Stockholm in three weeks he says will blow the lid off the sanctions failures and how too many at the top of several governments are skimming oil profits off the top and which companies are getting kickbacks. His speech will be the closing shot across the bow at the Global Environmental Responsibility Forum and is expected to bring in a huge international audience of protesters. Because of its importance Lina is scheduled to meet him as doting daughter who misses her papa. More likely she's there to soften his impact, make it clear her security is based on his not embarrassing the state. She will be heavily guarded of course, it's her presence in Russia that keeps him silent. Until now. I'm hearing chatter that certain people do not want it to be heard at all. They fear he would be a lightning rod. Currently, he's a small but respected fish in this pond. If that speech goes forth on a live feed it would propel him onto the world stage. To some that cannot happen. He wants, I want, you to break Lina free after his speech and bring her here."

Joshua thought about this. "And I suppose he refused to stand down."

"If he goes through with the speech both will be in serious danger but he only cared about her safety. So I had to promise to protect her."

"They're not going to hand her over."

"She knows you, she'll come with you."

"You've confirmed this?"

"No. He hasn't been allowed to speak to her again. That's your job, to convince her."

"And Yevi?"

"He says he's willing to take his chances. He feels it's his duty to report this information. I tried to talk him out of it, publish it instead, but he feels if the worst happens it will be his legacy."

"Talk him out of doing his duty? That's hardly believable." Joshua regretted that as soon as he said it.

Bennett stiffened. "Why do you always underestimate me?"

"Underestimate? You manipulate the system better than anyone. Here I am as proof of that."

"Stop it! I asked you here as a professional, man to man. It's time for you to grow up. I understand that you have resentments. Maybe I failed as a parent but you're not a boy and some things are more important than your feelings."

If thoughts could combust Joshua would have burned the house down. But he had long been curious about his father's relationship to Yevi, it seemed far beyond school chums.

"Give me the details." He tried not to sound like a petulant schoolboy.

"And when it's finished, can we talk?"

"Talk?"

"Kellenstone was worried, of course he called. I spent days using every contact I had. Suddenly you call like nothing happened, asking me to give out a cover story that I was negotiating to free you from a Russian prison, under the radar. I doubt he believed me but was relieved enough to make it official, keep a lid on the news. The obvious question is why?"

"Why what?"

"Why propagate a story like that? Why not just return?"

"It's complicated."

"You involved me. And Monroe, for that matter. You can explain the complicated. Stop acting like a spoiled brat, I'm tired of it."

"And I'm tired of a father who never was."

"Oh, right, poor little rich boy, neglected while I ran a business. Stop feeling sorry for yourself, you made yourself a legend so congratulations and can we for once talk like normal human beings?"

"That's the problem, things were never normal between us."

Bennett started to respond then left the room as Gerry's wife Edith rushed in and enveloped Joshua in one of her blissful hugs. Joshua loved his surrogate parents deeply but always knew they worked for and cared as deeply for his father. Still, it was good to be back in familiar arms.

"What do you have in the oven? Something I hate eating, no doubt, too many vegetables, you always make too many vegetables, Aunt Edie."

She had to reach high to pat him on the cheek as if he were still a boy, as to her he probably was. "You must eat your vegetables. They will make you strong."

He laughed. "And so they did. Can't you see?" He twirled her once around, surprised at how much he'd missed her. She more than anyone had gotten him through those dark days. And years. He quickly erased his feelings, still unsure what had happened at the Knezevic farm when he felt he might pass out and not wanting a repeat. Especially not here.

She gasped. "Your face? What happened to your face? That is a scar, not maybe healed yet." She glared at him, what was he doing with himself?

"It was nothing. Your vegetables made me too tall and I bumped into a tree branch."

Uncle Gerry knew better and by his expression knew that nothing was resolved with his father. He had always hoped father and son would reconcile; still, he was here, maybe it was the opening he'd always hoped for.

"Do not you lie to me. Master Joshua. Or my meatloaf will stay in the kitchen."

"Then I'll eat with you and Uncle Gerry in the kitchen."

Gerard spoke, firmly. "No, Joshua. You will eat with your father. And you will wait until after to discuss business. It's not good for digestion."

Joshua starts to disagree, looking to Edith to back him up even as he knew she would never go against her husband.

Frowning like the reprimanded schoolboy he once was he headed for the dining room where his father was already sitting at the head of a long table, set for two, nursing a small Scotch.

"Drink?"

"No, I'm driving." Any hopes of his staying over were put to rest. Bennett nodded, he'd expected as much.

81

Edith, a cheery partner to Gerard's wise but sometimes dour countenance, brought in her specialty meat loaf, a simple meal but Joshua's favorite from boyhood. Mashed potatoes, mushy peas and sauteed baby carrots with onions and honey; the aroma of a cooling apple pie on the credenza filled the room. Edith believed a happy stomach could prevent wars, it was hunger that begat all problems. She was younger than her husband when she was hired as part-time kitchen help but her father having early on left the family she'd been sent out to work as soon as legally allowed. She immediately set her eyes on Gerard Francis O'Leery. He was at first chagrined then flattered but ultimately she, and her proven true belief, had won the day. Ten years later they married at the estate. Bennett gave her away and paid for their honeymoon in Belfast, his boyhood home. Both thought of Joshua as their own having dedicated their world to Daine House. Young girls today just didn't eat, what were they thinking? Edith's gradual roundness, she felt, only enhanced her well being.

Knowing the tension that would fill the room she made her small talk about how good to have him back and my, how he'd grown as if not realizing he'd left school years before. Her husband finally caught her eye and insisted she leave them to it.

They ate in silence for a few minutes, neither particularly hungry but both going through the motions.

"Valerie was captured, my fault. I had to find her."

"I doubt it was your fault. I heard rumors but I knew nothing about her capture." He didn't add he wasn't as concerned, that was agency business.

"They found us… too easy, it was an ambush but I didn't know who or why. The assignment came from Kellenstone, by the way." He waited for his father's response.

"I know. He said he'd received information from an informant back in the day, that an old file was uncovered but didn't say what was in it. At great risk he photocopied, urgent retrieval or it would be easily traced back. I can tell you I've known him a long time and he would rather cut off an arm than sacrifice one of his team. He knows risk is part of the job, he feels his is to minimize that. He would have trusted his source before sending in one of his."

"Well, either he failed or his intel did. The restaurant was a last minute change of plans but a waiter was prepared for us. We got away but some local thugs were right behind. I escaped, Val didn't and I needed to find her."

Much calmer than he felt, Bennett said, "You were shot."

He shrugged. "I was laid up for a while. I didn't know where she was so I used a contact of yours, Sergey Kominsky or rather his son. Sergey died two years ago, natural causes they said. His son Ivan was willing to play. I paid well and said it was your orders and he would have a friend, should it be needed."

Bennett stared, dumbfounded.

"He went into town and was followed back. I thought he'd sold me out but from his expression he had no idea. I was in a hurry so I turned tables and offered money, to find out where she was. I'd get her and we'd find out who was behind it. Before I could learn anything…."

"I know. Kellenstone hinted she was safe, anything more was off limits, especially when you returned. You were safe, I didn't pursue the details. But know this, I will never let you rot in a foreign prison. The fact it was a cover story is irrelevant. You are my son whether you like it or not. You can't choose when it's handy and then dismiss. Now you're here and so is she. Under wraps, off limits to you."

"She is my partner. She is not off limits."

Bennett sighed, not a battle he would win."That's the official line. Just be careful. If what you say is true, it's what Monroe suspected, a rabid bat in the cave, as he put it. He can't find a thing to corroborate, though, and he's the best at it. So be careful. This is your father speaking, like it or not. Maybe Dr. Cheng can put some sense into you."

Joshua looked up. "A nice touch, that, what's it called? Intense resocializing?"

"It was that or a lockdown and that would have done you no good. She's the best in her field. I've known her for years. Don't look at me like that, she's not reporting to me."

"That's one thing in her favor."

"It was Monroe's idea, soften the edges. He believed you, but there's more to it, nothing he could or would share. Just be careful now. Don't go off...."

Joshua stood, ready to leave.

Bennett also stood, almost as tall, man to man. "I told Yevi I was thinking of retiring, it's not the same anymore. You must know that. The rules, the players, more volatile, have changed, our allies are unsure, and scared. I managed to pull in old favors but the loyalties have shifted. At least you're home, alive. But after we finish in Stockholm, I want you here, permanent."

"We?"

"I told Yevi I would be there, as a guest, no more. The assignment is yours. Then I want you to give up field work. I know you don't want to follow in my footsteps but I want to know you're safe. Field work has a shelf life, even for the best."

"Someone is behind this. I'll get Lina out for you but don't tell me how to run my life. It's way too late for fatherly advice."

"If you'd settle down and have children you'd realize it's never too late for that." He tried but failed to keep the sarcasm out of his voice.

"And work for Daine Investments, too? Anything else you want?" He didn't try to keep the sarcasm out of his voice.

"I'll get you the files. If there's even a hint of trouble you call for help. I can get reinforcements over there fast. It might be a good idea in any event."

"No. I don't want to worry about two sets of guard dogs. I can take care of Lina's. If I need help, I'll get it. I'm serious, one whiff of your interference and I'm out."

"Fine, but keep me in the loop. He's my oldest and dearest friend, he's trusted me with his child's safety. I don't take that lightly."

"Why? What hold does he have on you? It's more than friendship, I've always known that."

"His parents and mine. That's a long story for another time."

Joshua shrugged. "I'm taking Edith's pie, no Euro baker can top her desserts."

To Bennett it was almost an apology, the first sliver of light his son had granted him in a very long time. But if he'd hoped for more it ended when Joshua spoke.

"I have to be somewhere."

"I know we haven't…. There are others, a new generation, trained in new technology."

Joshua stared at him, his expression dismissive of the term "others."

"Then at least don't be so reckless." He waved away Joshua's look. "I know you think you're invincible and if it weren't for Yevi, I wouldn't have… . New people, they frighten me." He paused. "Please, be mindful of that."

Joshua paused. His father waited but the moment passed.

"I'm late. Is Rod here? I need to talk to him first."

"He's in his quarters."

At the door Bennett said, "I'm serious, if something is going on, I want to know. Don't shut me out, I can help."

Joshua started to reply when Edith came rushing out with two huge bags she handed to him. "You will eat all the vegetables. You will promise me."

He leaned way down to kiss her on the cheek. "I promise, Aunt Edie."

"You do not lie to me, Master Joshua."

He laughed. "I never lie to you. And never about vegetables."

"So I made you the meatloaf and pie, some extras. You will need your strength."

"I will need it to carry all this food." He raised the bags, as if straining with the weight.

Edith beamed, all was right with her Master Joshua. Behind her Gerard looked less sure.

Bennett watched his son walk away. It may not be all he wanted but for now it would have to do. And soon they would have that talk, no more secrets.

# #

Rod Bernmeister sat across from the boss' son. Twenty minutes before he'd knocked on the door as if it were a completely normal visit. He knew of his movements as he had cameras placed around the estate. When the sensor lights went on he'd checked, surprised. He let him in, they shook hands, each aware of the other but had no real relationship as he worked for the father and they were estranged. Until, apparently, tonight.

He didn't introduce himself but said, "I need to upload something onto your computer."

As director of security for Daine's myriad investments and business interests he had a high tech office setup, attached but separate from his living quarters, with computer screens from an extensive array of CCTVs and global news, especially areas of unrest. It was staffed around the clock, usually ex-military needing a job to ease back into society, quiet enough to decompress but plenty of outdoor space to move about.

Bernmeister wasn't sure he liked the idea of the boss' son having access, a virus could attach even if Daine wasn't aware of it. Yet to refuse was not an option. He always kept older models in his private quarters, nothing of importance stored, good for random searches, and showed him to his personal work area, as sparse as the man himself.

Both men stared at the screen. Gibberish or rather, coded. Bernmeister had no idea what it was, planning to destroy the hard drive disk and dump that machine as soon as Daine left. But clearly Daine knew exactly what it was. Without a word he sat, apparently thinking.

Make yourself at home, thought Bernmeister, beginning to understand why father and son were not close. He knew he'd been having dinner at the main house, it was his job to know comings and goings. His arrival wasn't a surprise, he'd seen Daine go to his car, drop in some bags and turn back, but his presence was.

Minutes later his guest stood and said, "Thank you." At the door he turned. "I'll be using the cabin tomorrow." Need to know, he really was a spook.

Even if Bernmeister hadn't had a thing about rich boys who never knew empty pockets he would not have liked Joshua Daine. If he'd been Bennett Daine's son he'd be so grateful to be part of…   but he knew better than to go there. Fantasy thoughts did no good.

#   #

Chapter 6

Valerie's apartment building was in a block of nondescript buildings, one of many low rise units built to house mid-level government employees. Over time most had disappeared, replaced with taller, more land efficient dwellings. To a covert agent, however, elevators and floors of stairs did not offer optimum escape. She needed only a few basic amenities, one parking spot and most of all, privacy. It was also cheaper than the more modern nearby high rises with fancier facades and poolside networking for the upwardly mobile.

Workdays were bad enough but weekends were harsh. She had no friends, only a elderly woman next door who'd tried to engage her but soon realized it was going to happen. Occasionally she could go into the office, at least it gave her something to do, but generally it was not encouraged. Why did anyone want to work when they didn't have to and weren't getting paid overtime? The C.I.A. was by nature suspicious and so she filled time searching through obscure journals online for any information she deemed useful. She struggled to avoid memories, knowing any thoughts of how she came to be here and she'd let out a scream that would only make her situation worse. She sometimes ran in the woods, going deep into areas most considered unsafe but in her present state of mind she almost welcomed an attack. Someone to beat the crap out of fit her mood perfectly. Alternate weekends she went to different shooting ranges outside the DC suburbs. They'd taken her gun and she didn't want to explain why she needed to keep up her skills. They would know she considered her position temporary and they'd made it clear it was not. If her superiors were aware it was not known to her.

She turned on the light and made her way to the kitchen and set her takeout meal on the counter. She'd given little thought to furnishing her small rental, it had come with a bed, sofa and TV. Previous tenants had left a cheap table and she'd taken a bookcase left by the dumpster, never bothering to paint it.. She'd added nothing but clean linens and a few kitchen items from a garage sale but otherwise her space was as sparse as the day she moved in.

She opened a bottle of wine and let it sit while she took a quick shower, changed into pajama bottoms and oversized worn tee. She rinsed a drinking glass in the sink then put the food carton and wine bottle on the coffee table, turning on the small TV to a series set in Hawaii, at least someone was having a good time. She filled the glass with wine and sat on the garishly flowered sofa, plumped a pillow on her lap and put the carton on top. Barely tasting the food, she washed it down with a hefty swig, blotting out how her exciting life of an agent had gone so far downhill.

Hours later, the food and wine on the coffee table having at least managed to be put there before she fell asleep on the sofa, the late news was on. There was not much of a moon and only a lone dog walker in pajamas and overcoat. A battered jeep pulled up and squeezed into a parking spot too close to a hydrant. No one noticed or cared, everyone was indoors sleeping, getting high or making love. If one wanted a brief description of the inhabitants it would be predictable.

She stirred, blinked a few times then poured another glass of wine, clicked off the TV and headed for the bedroom. Outside, barely visible from even inches away, someone watched the lights go out.

Valerie, in her bed, covers strewn, nearly empty glass on the nightstand, was in a wine induced sleep. A small beam from a streetlamp peeked through a slit in the curtains. A figure dressed in dark clothing, barely visible in the doorway, stood silently, taking in the wine glass, the restless sleep and the strewn clothing. Slowly he moved to the bed and sat, facing her.

Suddenly startled awake but before she could react a hand was placed over her mouth. She squirmed violently, more from anger than fear. "Mmmpphhh."

"Be fucking quiet!"

Her eyes widened in recognition of Joshua. His tone of voice stopped her immediately but when he eased off she hauled off to slug him although he easily managed to stop the blow. He pinned her down.

"Don't. We both know where that will go. I need to talk to you."

"I sent a message to you months ago. The Pony Express take the scenic route?"

"I was in a Russian prison."

That stopped her. "For real?"

"No, it's a cover. I was trying to find you."

"I was here. I still don't know how that happened. One minute some drooling piece of muscle was thanking his lucky stars, the next I was at an embassy, showered and sent home to be tortured."

"You have an office job."

"Like I said."

She lay back, tried to focus. All she could muster was a feeble, "So? No phones? Telegraph? Smoke Signal?"

He laughs, lays down next to her. "I've missed you."

"They wouldn't tell me where you were. Alive or dead. Nothing." She wanted to cry but it wasn't in her ability so anger was her stock substitute. "Why are you here? I mean now? Rather than say, knock on the door like real people? Let me know you were okay? Something. And don't expect me to believe you, just like that, as I remember you lie better than anyone I've ever met. In fact, I think I trained you in it."

"Good to know you haven't changed." A slight hint of sarcasm. "Get dressed. Make it fast. We need to be somewhere before daylight."

"Just like that? How dare you…." But she knew him and knew he meant it. She crawled out of bed, rubbing her head. "Well, go make coffee, it's not showtime." He walked out, she didn't see his smile.

#   #

As the sun began to gray the horizon with it's first glow the battered black jeep wound through a mountainous terrain devoid of traffic or any moving object except for a deer running across the road ahead. After a few more curves and an unpaved road it pulled up to a simple log cabin, well hidden in a forest of trees, and stopped off to the side.

Valerie slid more than stepped out, and stretched. "How long did it take you to find the most uncomfortable ride since that train in Istanbul, the one that broke down every two miles?"

"Fancy rides in the country get noticed. Just because we're home doesn't mean we get to go stupid."

"You always were the romantic one."

Under his breath, "I know."

"What?"

"Take the bags inside, I'll hide the Jeep." He tossed out two carryalls, leaving her to glare but do as told.

Inside the cabin, nicer than expected from such a simple exterior, it had a full kitchen, upgraded appliances and an eating counter in addition to a built in booth that could seat six. A bedroom door could be seen with a full bed, made up. Two large pristine sofas and easy chairs surrounded a rock fireplace. Books lined a series of shelves.

He entered, immediately setting the alarm code.

"This is the Daine version of roughing it?"

"Something like that. But walls are secure and motion sensor outside goes to a master at the house." He put bags of food in the fridge.

She checked the one bedroom, turned and pointed."Those are sleeper sofas, I take it. At least you'll be comfortable."

He looked at her. "I have something for your hangover."

She glared, searching for a retort but her head hurt too much. She settled on disinterest.

He busied himself in the kitchen for a few moments then handed her a glass of an indeterminate substance. "Family recipe. I can vouch for it."

She paused, still unable to think of a retort and took the glass. He went to the cabinet and handed her two aspirin. She took those and swallowed it all quickly, to avoid the taste. If she was grateful he'd never know it.

"Long night. We take a nap and then we talk."

She was too tired to argue, passing out as soon as her head hit the pillow. Joshua watched her then arranged the pillows on the sofa and lay down, allowing himself to finally feel his relief at finding her, safe and almost back to her old self. He was instantly asleep.

Just after noon he opened the bedroom door, carrying a glass.

"Get up. We're going out."

"What the…?"

"Drink up. I'll give you five minutes. This is a protein shake, should hold you till dinner."

She tried for a murderous stare but it came out bleary eyed and blinking.

"Drink or go hungry, your choice. I need to know what kind of shape you're in. I'm guessing there's work to do."

Outside, two hours later, one of them was enjoying the sing song sounds of nature. To Joshua, having found Valerie he was in his element, outdoors, free of constraints, all right with his world. To her, doing her best to not let him see her struggle as they hiked uphill, her feelings were decidedly mixed. He was not dead but in her present misery, if she could just catch her breath, she thought that might not last.

"Good. You're in better shape than I thought. You haven't completely let go."

If that was a compliment it missed. Oddly, she liked him all the more for it.

"I'll see you back at the cabin." He disappeared from sight in a matter of seconds.

Near sunset she returned, having taken her time hoping to annoy him but instead found him in the kitchen setting out eating utensils. She felt better than willing to admit.

"I have leftover meatloaf, a full roasted chicken and way too many vegetables. Apple pie for dessert."

"Why are we here? If you're sorry you left me stranded and practically tortured in a foreign prison, flowers would have been fine."

"You were seen leaving in an embassy car."

"They told me you were dead."

"Nothing I could do about that. I had other business."

"Good to know your priorities are so warm and fuzzy."

"You were fine, okay?" He looked at her.

Weeks of forgettable meals, she couldn't take her eyes off the food. "Maybe a drumstick."

He loaded up the plates and carried them to the table. She washed her hands then sat while he returned for the wine bottle, looked at her, put it down and opened the fridge for a pitcher and took the water to the table and filled her glass.

"Based on your kitchen your eating habits have deteriorated."

She frowned at the water. "You're the food police now?"

"Well trained, by the best. Eat all your vegetables."

She stared at him. Something was wrong, she could smell it. That or the apple pie, being reheated in the oven. Still, no sense turning away good food. She ate, waiting for him to get to his point.

"Seriously, who knew carrots could taste good?" She placed heaping seconds on her plate. "Is there ice cream to go with that pie?"

He watched her, silent at how terrified he'd been until he'd found out she was desk bound. He knew she'd hate that, more than any punishment but to him it meant she was safe. And that was all that mattered.

For the first time it occurred to him that maybe he understood his father's concern and maybe even his absence from his life. He'd kept his son safe; the O'Leery's took very good care of him and the boarding school had taught him discipline and sports.

Some things mattered more than others.

Without warning, his head began to spin. This time he recognized a flashback and the last thing he wanted was for her to know.

"I'll be back in a minute, get something from jeep."

He rushed out, leaving her to cross over and take the pie out of the oven and check the freezer for ice cream. Bingo. She started to scoop it up when it occurred to her that something had happened, something really was wrong. She put down the scoop. No more waiting for him to fill her in, they were partners, they told all.

She went outside, quietly, wondering what direction he'd gone. It was completely dark, no moon light. She knew it wasn't the jeep, he didn't forget things. She saw a clump of trees past the clearing and headed over. Before she was two steps in he grabbed her and pulled her close. He said nothing.

He had remembered a time at school when his father had come to visit, before the first Christmas break. His female assistant was in the car and Joshua jumped to the conclusion he had replaced his mother. He was furious. His father told him Gerard would pick him up at the break and bring him to Switzerland, he was leaving that day for a conference but would be free to spend the holiday with him.

Joshua refused to go. He said he'd made friends and had his own plans. His father could have insisted, of course, but he didn't. Joshua spent most of the school break in his room, alone. He never knew if Gerard told his father. Eventually he'd learned she was his translator, nothing more, but it didn't resolve the anger he'd felt that day.

Valerie let him hold on to her; she knew he'd been as frightened as she was by what had happened. Together they had a friction that kept them focused on work but over time, learning to rely on each other, had built an unbreakable bond. A potential loss was part of the game, drilled into them in training. She'd had to debrief when she returned and been forced to accept his loss for the record. Her assignment to desk duty forced her to cope within the lines at all times but her insides felt as if they'd been eviscerated.

Abruptly, he pulled his arms away. "We have to talk. Not now, it's been, well, let's get some sleep, tomorrow."

They returned to the cabin.

#   #

Sunday morning chirping birds greeted the day and the brightness of the early sunlight streamed through the windows. Joshua was up and dressed, in the kitchen. A pitcher of orange juice was on the counter with two coffee cups, plates and utensils. Coffee percolated, filling the cabin with its rich aroma.

He walked to the bedroom door and knocked. "I'm coming in." He didn't wait for an answer but opened it. Valerie was in bed, bleary-eyed but awake.

"Breakfast in ten."

"Go away. I haven't slept in a bed this comfortable since before I met you. You never take me to the best places."

"Hurry up. We have to talk."

She threw a pillow in his direction but it landed on the floor beside the bed. With a groan, she moved aside the covers. He left her to it.

Ten minutes later, barefoot, she staggered out, still in oversize pajamas, wearing a man's robe, open. Her hair was tamed on one side. He had tongs in one hand, a spoon in the other facing a griddle and frying pan on top of the stove. He opened the oven and pulled out a tray of biscuits, his feast of a breakfast now ready.

"Aren't we fresh as a fucking daisy?"

"What?"

"Nothing. Are we expecting company?"

"No. English boarding school days. Always have breakfast, never know what the day will bring."

"I meant, I didn't know you could cook."

"There are a lot of things you don't know about me."

"As your partner of way too long, I appreciate the honesty."

"You need to build up your strength."

She glared. "Really? You're taking inventory now?"

He turned, softened his tone somewhat. "We have a long day ahead. And a lot of catching up to do. We may have trouble."

"In that case fill 'er up." She handed over an empty coffee cup.

She shuffled across and slid into the booth, sipping the hot coffee. Under her breath, she said, "Probably ground the beans, too."

He joined her with two heaping plates. She looked appalled at so much food so early. "I'm good with just coffee, thanks. We never had this much food in one place all the years we worked together. I'm not going to start now."

"Eat it. You've let yourself go and we have work to do."

"That's it? I got jammed onto a desk job, no one would tell me why or said a word about you, so yeah, I had issues. I notice you look terrific, that Russian prison you weren't in must have agreed with you."

"I was shot." He points to the scar on his forehead, healed but still visible. "I thought you'd have asked about it by now."

She stared at it, releasing emotions buried since her release. She got up, ran to the bedroom and slammed the door shut. Behind the door she took in gulps of air until she gained control.

Joshua watched her go, began to wonder again if his father was right. This job took a toll. He waited to see if another flashback came over him and was much relieved when it didn't. He took both plates, wrapped them in foil and placed in the oven.

An hour later she returned, showered, hair in place and clean clothes.

"I'm hungry."

Another hour later, plates pushed aside, she sipped her coffee and said, "Are you sure it was a set up? Stealing documents from a foreign embassy comes with some risk." Which is why they sent me, she didn't add.

"No one knew the cafe was a drop-off, last minute change of plans. Someone knew of those changes."

"I don't know, Joshua. That waiter, he…."

"Had a gun, knew where you'd be. And he was already there, you weren't followed. If not set up then a leak, a mole, something. Look, I don't know how or why yet, I just know when something is very wrong. You have to trust me on this."

He handed over the thumb drive. "Someone is going to a lot of trouble for this. It's encoded. The only computers with the older version of this program is likely at H.Q., probably in that underground storage area but access is restricted. Any ideas?"

She thought a minute. "I might have. I mean, I work with some serious geeks."

"You can't use anyone working there. Not yet anyway. I'm serious, until we know what's on it, keep it hidden."

"What you're saying is one of the good guys is not one of the good guys."

"Maybe. Someone is sharing intel, that's what I'm saying. So don't go sneaking around with this until we know who's watching. Deal?"

She started to argue but stopped. "Deal. Hand over that last biscuit and the jelly. You're probably right, I'm going to need my strength."

His phone vibrated. She proceeded to butter the biscuit and slab on the jelly while he listened. From his expression the news wasn't good.

"Right. You take care of the rest." He hung up. "Grab your stuff."

She dropped the biscuit, went to fetch her carryall, packed and ready, from the bed. When she returned he had a door panel open behind the fireplace, well hidden.

"Follow this out, someone will meet you. Go back to work as if nothing happened. And don't do anything until I contact you."

"But...."

"Now!"

She disappeared behind the fireplace.

He cleared the table, pans and dishes went into the dishwasher, not carefully. He looked around, sure all traces of her were gone then grabbed his carryall, set the alarm and walked leisurely to the jeep, hidden under a canopy of shrubs.

He looked up. In the distance a dot appeared in the sky. He set the carryall on the seat and pulled off the back. Hidden inside was a high powered rifle. He moved nearer the clearing to get a better aim, waited for the drone to move closer and fired a round of shots. The drone exploded, raining down.

He watched, wondering who would send a drone on recon to his father's home. Were they searching for something specific, like him, or anything that could be useful? That he was being tracked wasn't a surprise, his return had already set off concerns, he knew that.

The explosion, however, was a surprise. That meant the drone was altered to leave no trace should it be shot out of the air or rammed into something. A very dangerous thing with attached explosives; it meant ancillary damage was not a concern.

He briefly checked the surrounding area for any signs that intruders had penetrated. More from habit as he didn't expect to find anything, Rod would have it covered. Had someone learned the location? Were they followed? Was Valerie being watched to find him? Or was the plan to map the Daine estate?

The computer file he'd given to her was important to someone. He had to find a way into the graveyard, as the storage of old computers full of decades of secrets was known. Ordinarily that would have been easy but now he didn't know who to trust.

He'd made sure his partner was safe. Now he began to wonder if the trip to Stockholm was connected, the timing seemed more than coincidental.

Further back in the forest Valerie exited a narrow opening in a hidden rock formation and paused to check her locale. The tunnel was about two hundred feet and ended in a patch of heavy foliage. Met by whom, she wondered as she heard the explosion. Her instinct was to race to the sound. She dropped her bag and pulled her gun from behind her belt just as a hand grabbed her arm. She looked into the face of Rod Bernmeister, Bennett Daine's driver and bodyguard. He wasn't much taller than she was but she could tell his body was as solid as cement covered with skin. His grip was an iron vise.

"Who are you?"

"My orders are to see you get safely home without anyone knowing you were gone."

"Explosive device mean anything?"

"He can take care of himself, you must know that by now."

"I don't take orders from you."

"We take orders from the same person. Does anyone call or check on you?"

"No. I usually go out running on weekends."

"Not today, your car is still there."

"How did…?"

"Questions don't work for me. You return after dark, act like you slept all day. How hard is that?"

She didn't like him. What was his connection to Joshua? Another piece of information she didn't know about him.

#   #

Monday morning Valerie headed to the parking area behind her apartment. She was off her game after a restless night, dressed for an early run before work. Joshua had turned up safe, which both relieved and infuriated her. She saw he was fine and was given her part to play but she also had no idea what she was looking for. And neither did he, apparently. Going in

103

blind was never a good plan but it was the best they had. That didn't mean she liked it.

And what was that about removing some Russian's daughter from Sweden after a speech? Was that business or something more? She realized how little her partner shared even within their confines of need to know. He wanted her complete trust but seemed to come up short for himself.

She stopped behind her car to do warm-up stretches and to check the area. She'd paid extra to be assigned the last stall, force of habit to not be visible from any windows. A neighbor walked out with his dog. The dog strained its leash to sniff her, the owner said "sorry" without meaning as he jerked back his dog and walked on. She watched him go then thoroughly checked again before she got in her car and drove off.

She'd spent the day before mostly furious. Hard to imagine a man more annoying than Joshua; they must be related. Rod something - he'd put a contact number in her phone "for emergency only" - and had taken her to what she supposed was a safe house. She was told to stay put, he had things to do and would pick her up later. If she tried to go outside an alarm would sound and she would no longer be alone. There was food. He left without saying goodbye.

She looked around. Definitely a Daine property, well stocked, indeed. Five star hotels could come there and weep.

Bernmeister returned well after dark. One look at his face and she chose not to argue. In silence they drove to her block where he parked several doors down but didn't turn off the engine.

"He said to give you this. Hide it."

A prepaid phone. She stuck it in her satchel.

"I trust you can get inside without being seen?"

"I could have done that at noon." She grabbed her bag and got out without looking back.

# #

Chapter 7

A light drizzle had ruined her outing and traffic would be backed up so she might as well take her time getting ready, give herself time to think. Running was for clearing the head not filling it. It took her a few minutes of feeling something not quite right before she noticed she was headache free. She'd reached for the ubiquitous bottle of aspirin when she realized she didn't need it. She'd fallen asleep without her usual wine chaser, or three. One more thing for which to be pissed off at Joshua who no doubt saw himself as her sobriety coach. As if by his osmosis she'd even stuffed her carryall with food from the safe house fridge, roasted chicken with potatoes, onions and carrots, no sense letting it go to waste.

Act normal at work, he'd told her. Work, under Melissa Gallagher directly and Monroe Kellenstone above that, specifically the Office of Financial Irregularities, C.I.A., a benign title for tracking worldwide criminals who have to hide their money somewhere and then make it clean enough to move into the legal system. Money from illegal activities had to flow through the financial chain. Banks face a great deal of scrutiny and it's no easy task to hide millions and sometimes billions without someone noticing the piggy bank was full from no known source. Downhill from there, to all sorts of other dark corners. Sure, a zillion legal loopholes to lessen financial impact but if reported as required how do you say drug kingpin or human trafficker or secret arms dealing under occupation in ways that won't bring the Feds knocking? Without a legitimate business to run it through a network of lessened scrutiny is required and that, of course, takes money. Each step becomes a bread crumb along a winding trail back to the source.

Before he'd showed up and ruined a perfectly miserable weekend she'd gotten on to a thread of money that was tied to a U.S. bank. Not the usual high amounts but enough to catch her attention except she couldn't sort why. Now the memory swooped in like an eagle on a rabbit.

Usually the money they tracked was buried within several foreign entities. Too many banks around the world owed their strong balance sheets to ill gotten gains. On some days it seemed like all of them but she knew that was untrue; those who played by the rules in today's fast moving markets deserved a special award for just being honest in the face of such temptation. Or maybe they weren't so arrogant as to think her department couldn't find them and exchange their upscale digs for a not so comfy jail cell.

She knew a lot about that. Her father had died in jail. He'd thought he could handle market fluctuations and come out ahead and that borrowing from his investors to pay off losses could be easily made up. Gambling with other people's money rarely ended well and it didn't for him.

Until it all crashed down it had been a perfect life. Two children, an adored older brother who'd committed suicide after two years of constant media innuendos, his job and marriage in ruins, no money and no prospects. Her mother, a high maintenance high spending wife of a successful financial investment lawyer now alternated between denial and victim. They all shared common space if not common values in a big house in Connecticut. She went to the best schools, decent if not stellar grades, Dartmouth College until her junior year where she changed her major from English to French literature after playing Fantine in *Les Misérable*s by Victor Hugo. She'd forged a plan to live and work in Paris after graduation, a peripatetic writer or maybe a star of *Comédie Française*, soon to be a recipient of great talent and fame.

The irony of having tasted fame from the wrong side, which then morphed into a life where her survival often depended on no fame but left her fulfilled and challenged, escaped her.

She'd been away when the F.B.I. had raided their home. Her mother called, hysterical, she had to rush home. Valerie had no intention of doing that, her mother was often hysterical. She got off the phone then went about her day. Before her roommate had returned with that awful look on her face was the last time she'd been happy.

Until she met Joshua Daine.

Partnered with him, traveling through Europe, clandestine meets with allies, grabbing information for the security services, it was a life she felt born to, her past life relegated to a blur of hazy memories.

After her father's final hearing, guilty on all counts, thirty-six years minimum, she'd rushed out of the courtroom to find somewhere she could collapse. Their home was in foreclosure, her mother still trying to salvage something to maintain her lifestyle when none of her friends wanted anything to do with her and her own personal savings for her life in Paris, all gone. The cameras that clicked away like locusts devouring crops were barely heard. At the street, blinded by tears, she had turned to run when someone stepped in front and blocked her.

She was ready to fight, she could not deal with another reporter in her face, when he showed her a badge. Filled with dread, had they found something on her, was there more, she couldn't take any more. She'd almost fainted. He was quick, caught her arm to steady.

"Here, get in the car. You can catch your breath. I promise I don't bite and I don't have a camera."

She'd let him put her inside the maroon Ford, even as she considered he might be a serial killer or something but at that moment she didn't really care.

The car took off, leaving reporters in the dust. When she'd gathered enough of her wits, she looked at him. He was decent looking, probably in his fifties, short hair, decent suit, bland tie, dark eyes and gray hair.

"My name is Daniel Stephenson. I work for the C.I.A.. And I'd like to make you an offer."

Her eyes widened. "I'm not spying on my Dad. I didn't know anything then and I don't now. I only went to court because, well, I needed to hear it all. My mother just keeps crying about how awful her life is and my brother hasn't spoken in weeks. I'm done with it all. I don't care what your offer is. Let me out." She banged at the car door, the lock controlled up front.

"Sorry, you're not a prisoner but I can't let you jump into traffic. Tyrick, pull over when you can."

A few blocks later the car stopped. "At least listen to what I have to say. If the answer is no, you can get out here. I'll even give you taxi fare. Although we do run background checks and I know you have nowhere to go. You have one kind elderly neighbor letting you stay but her family wants you out, believing like father like daughter. I'm offering you room and board, a place to work out some of your anger and maybe after a while, a career opportunity."

She stared at him, mouth open. It hardly made sense. "How legal is this? I've had my fill of courts and federal cops so what you say better not have a whiff of anything funny. But I'll listen."

A silent nod and the car moved back into traffic and to the home of her neighbor without asking her for directions, where she had retrieved her belongings after having insisted they stop for food to bring her, the least she could do, an advance on her salary, if he was legitimate. He smiled, gave Tyrick the name of a restaurant where they all sat, ate and talked, her first full meal in, well she wasn't sure. Even more to her surprise, she was ravenous. They each had coffee but waited patiently until she'd finished. Stephenson remembered to add the takeout.

And so it began. She'd left a recorded message on her mother's phone that she was moving, had no way of contacting her brother, and off she went into training. Room and board was a bit lofty for the dorms and commissary but for a person on the run as she thought of herself, the physical workouts, brutal and thorough, the classroom training after, it suited. They already knew she had proficiency in languages, one of her professor's had a contact, occasionally sent prospective names, how they locked on to her. Her background, which she'd thought should have disqualified her actually gave her undercover stories some validity. Read up on her and easy to believe she was ready to infiltrate or join or be somewhere else. If she had money, well of course her father would have left an offshore account for her.

Always a bit of a drama queen she'd often manipulated her friends and parents to get what she wanted. She quickly learned that once she'd locked on to the assigned character she simply became that person. Isn't that what she'd wanted for real? To be someone else, someone whose father hadn't destroyed her family and her existence? She'd been given a new life, to pretend it was hers soon became the same thing to her.

She'd traveled the world enjoying the challenge and yes, the risks. Her previous world as she knew it had no meaning because she had no family, no one to care about her one way or the other.

Her partner became that family but now she wondered if it were true for him. Yet to lose Joshua was to lose everything all over again. She would not let that happen.

# #

At her desk she folded into her usual workday slump. No one noticed her slightly late arrival, maybe it wasn't the first time, she couldn't remember. Today though, something on her computer screen was troubling. Normally she'd pass it along to Missy, to share with the others for a deeper dive. But Joshua had said to be careful. He didn't know who or what and he was off, maybe headed to Sweden already, some international economic climate change gathering of those who gave a damn about the planet. Certainly not the current administration; to them it was about money and nothing else.

It was only a thread but threads once pulled can unravel a lot of secrets. A cursory check and she knew she was staring at something bigger. Caution, though, no one could know what she'd found and that was tricky in a department where everyone unearthed secrets. She'd have to find a back door to search while seemingly unearthing something completely different.

Finally, from the dreary life of a desk jockey she was forced to endure, a challenge. Like a field agent she would play the part and play it well. No more going through the motions, that moment began her interest in following the money trail.

Valerie hadn't realized the day was over until the person at the next desk, a twenty something nerd who really needed to see a skin doctor and wash his hair more often but was otherwise a decent chap who didn't clutter her day with needless pleasantries, nudged her.

"You have to come up for air sometime, you know."

"What?" She glanced at the photo I.D. card hanging from his neck. Derek Applegate.

"It's after seven. Missy has been staring at you for the past half hour. She wants to leave but wonders what you're on about, glued to your screen like you're counting YouTube visits."

"YouTube?" She had no idea what he was talking about.

"Trust me on this. Shut down your computer now and laugh at something I said."

She stared at him.

"Okay, I get it, pretend to laugh at something I said. Then point to something on your screen and I'll shake my head no. Then shut down your computer and we'll walk out together. You're being watched and I'm saving your ass. Now go."

Something in his voice and thinking he would not do this just to mess with her, she smiled, a laugh would be out of character. Then she pointed to the screen, he looked over and shook his head. She shrugged and turned off her computer, stretched and casually pulled out her purse. Derek stood, waiting for her. She managed to look surprised at his behavior and as if reluctant, stick to the same behavior, she rarely left with anyone, they walked out. She stopped to get her coat, he waited, she looked annoyed but went with him.

In the elevator, knowing there were cameras she continued looking annoyed. He said, "Do you have dinner plans?"

"Yes."

"Oh."

They continued in silence. In the parking garage she whispered, "What the fuck was that all about?"

"You can thank me later. Missy was watching you like a cougar that just spotted dinner. You hadn't taken your eyes off the computer screen in hours and she suspects something. I was just giving you some cover so you can make up a story. Because she's going to ask you about it. She doesn't like surprises. So over your fake dinner plans you should fake up a story for why you're not sharing with the rest of us."

"Why are you helping me?"

"Because I'm stuck here instead of jail for hacking into a few, well, let's say Homeland Security and Goldman Sachs could have better security firewalls." He paused. "And you don't treat me like I'm a snake among the mice."

"Honestly, I didn't know that about you."

"Honesty, an overrated quality. But you treat everyone as if they don't exist. You didn't try to get a desk that didn't include me next to you."

"You mind your own business, what's not to like?" She smiled. "And thanks. I'll try to… uh… be more…."

"Yeah, right. Don't overdo it. And I don't like Missy. I don't trust her."

"Why?"

"Dunno. Reminds me of the woman that took my Dad away, I guess."

"I'm sorry. About your dad. Men are stupid sometimes."

"Yeah. Thanks. See you tomorrow. If you need a wing man, uh, I mean on your story for Missy, let me know."

"I will. And Derek, thanks. I'm glad you're not in jail."

He smiled. He had really nice teeth. A few more years and he'd be a decent looking man with a big salary. He'd be fine.

"So's my mom."

# #

The next day at her desk Valerie, beavering away, did not notice Missy until she loomed over her. Rage was not a good look on her, blue eyes do not have the same intensity as brown and the effect was not the same. She glanced at Derek, he shrugged. She'd told him her story was that she was following a mid level congressional staffer who was suddenly throwing money around local night spots. It was quickly determined that he was recently divorced from a wealthy woman and been paid off to not mention she had a girlfriend but for her purposes it would do.

"Good morning. Something I can help you with?"

"My office. Now."

Slowly but not so slow as to irritate her, Valerie followed. Missy shut the door, closed the curtains and then sat at her desk.

"Sit. We're going to have a chat."

Valerie sat. "Obviously you have something on your mind. Care to share or were you planning to intimidate me. I'll save you time, it won't work."

"Don't start. I'm not your problem although I can be."

"Take a deep breath and start at the beginning."

She glowered some more, it almost made Valerie want to laugh. She had a brief flashback to her interrogator, ugly and huge and nasty, willing to kill on a nod from a superior. Missy could not top that although to be honest, she wasn't completely sure about the killing part.

"You've been seeing Joshua Daine." She made it sound like she was accusing her of trying to steal her boyfriend. Although boyfriend might not be the correct word. Valerie wondered if her love life was a secret around here. Maybe she should go out for drinks with the team more often.

"He's my partner."

"Was. Was your partner. He's off limits to you."

"Why?"

"Why anything around here? Someone up high said so. He's been compromised."

"I doubt that. He would let them kill him before he'd turn."

"Then where is the flash drive?"

That surprised Valerie although she didn't change her expression. She thought quickly. "It was in the bag that got left at the scene."

"No, it wasn't."

That really surprised her. How would Missy know that? She was beginning to fit some pieces together and they weren't pretty.

"Then maybe it was lost. Or stolen."

"Not that either."

Valerie stared, blank faced. "Well, I don't have it. And if Joshua has it then he's turned it over. That was the assignment."

"Actually, he didn't. We set him up with Dr. Cheng to see if she could get it out of him but he's not a big talker."

"If you think he shares with me you're mistaken. He's a bank vault with information."

"Then where is he? The orders are to bring him in, one way or another." She paused. "If you want to save him, now is the time to tell us."

"Us?"

"Need to know."

"Well, sorry. I don't know. Off limits, remember?"

"Don't mess with me. He's back, he would have contacted you."

"Sure, we had tea, catching up on old times, you know how it goes. Need to know."

"Lie to me and you'll be branded an accessory."

"Accessory to what? Last I saw him was leaving that cafe. We got separated, I got captured, you got me out. Many thanks, by the way. Working here has just been a dream job."

Missy glared. "I'm sure you think you're clever but this is bigger than both of us. You'll do well to get clear of it."

"And you? How deep are you in it?"

"I work for people who run this country, as you'd be well advised to do."

"Tell me who ordered the hit on him and why."

"I didn't say he was being taken out."

"Really? Sounds to me like you did. And I want to know why. You're up to your eyeballs in dirty money. You want to know what I was doing? Following your little trail of offshore accounts. That's what got me suspicious, how easy it was to trace back to you. Not very well hidden considering where you work."

"What are you talking about?"

"Playing innocent is not your best color. I want to know what's going on with Joshua, who ordered the nonexistent hit, or an email with lots of juicy attachments will go out to a lot of news organizations."

"What attachments? I really have no idea what you're talking about. You're the one in trouble here, not me."

Valerie stared. She was telling the truth. This was not going at all well. She had to get to Joshua and fast but first she had to find out who was behind this. Whatever this was. Who wanted him out of the game? Well, a lot of people, he'd made many enemies but why now? What hadn't he told her? Something about a speech, she was trying to remember exactly but right now she had to get away from Missy who seemed to want him as much as she did.

"Fine. Bring it on. I've been sitting at that desk doing what I was told to do. Prove otherwise."

Her phone rang. She debated picking it up then grabbed it. "What?"

She listened, then said, "She's here, something about an offshore account in my name. What's that all about?"

She listened again. "I don't care. Fix it. Where can we meet? Yes, now."

Valerie strained to hear the voice at the other end but no luck before Missy slammed down the phone.

"We need to go somewhere more private, you seem to be trying to blackmail me. As your supervisor I feel we should get to know each other better. Share information, girl talk."

"I'm good, thanks. Maybe drinks after?"

Missy dropped her fake smile, reached into a drawer, pulled out a small weapon and set it on the desk. "It isn't a request."

As they walked out, Derek watched, curious. He looked around, no one else seemed to notice. He stretched, closed his files, got up and headed for the men's room. He heard the stairwell door shut, knew cameras would pick them up but that might be too late. He did a brief jog in place to warm up, for the watchers, and followed.

In the parking garage, Valerie, more curious than frightened, allowed Missy to take the lead. Was Missy the mole? She didn't seem to have thought it out particularly well meaning it could go either way. Missy's panic was emotional. Who was pulling her strings?

At a light blue late model Mercedes sedan, Missy said, "Get in or I'll shoot."

"Not to point out the obvious but we're in a C.I.A. parking garage and cameras are probably on us now. Smile."

"I found you in unauthorized files. You attacked me."

"Missy, you haven't thought this through. The files on my computer are your offshore accounts wired through an American bank with enough bread crumbs to feed a flock of migrating birds."

"That won't work on me. I told you. I don't know what you're talking about."

"Then try this. Killing me will make it murder not money laundering, big difference where you end up."

"Clearly you set me up."

Something in Missy's eyes made Valerie pause. She was hiding something but it wasn't money. "It was too easy to uncover. You can use that. You still have time to say it was your plan all along, to trap whomever might want you neutralized."

Missy stared at her. "You're lying. You're the one setting me up." But her voice lacked conviction this time.

"Why would I do that? Think, Missy, you're in it up to your $300 haircut. Your only chance is to get ahead of it. You'll lose your job but can still avoid treason charges."

"Just tell me where is the flash drive. I don't know what's on it. I only….. " When it hit her it hit hard.

"You only what?"

"When I went to Munich. I said I had an agent to pick up, that was you and…."

Valerie really wanted the rest of the story but for now she had to get moving.

"I want to know about Joshua. It's gone too far, you've been compromised, I'm between you and prison."

She was a quick thinker when it came to her protection. "Daine's father is going to Stockholm, some speech. He's going to be used as bait in exchange for the flash drive. When Daine goes after him, it was supposed to be you but Kellenstone sent me to get to you first. Then he disappeared, like he does. That son of a… I got you out, you owe me for that."

Valerie wanted to hit her, hard, just slightly less than she wanted more information. She signaled, keep going.

"I had to choose. Your job was to turn it over so he would know where it is." She was pleading now, playing the innocent victim.

"Who? Who is doing all this? Kellenstone?"

"No. You need to talk to…."

Before she could finish Missy dropped, the rifle crack came a split second later. Brain matter splashed on Valerie. She ignored that, stepped away in time to

121

see someone in dark clothing with a shoulder sack run away and took off after.

Just then Derek came out of the staircase, saw Valerie running and Missy on the ground, dead. Within seconds he was surrounded by four security guards, guns drawn.

"Wait! I can explain."

Or could have if he hadn't fainted.

#   #

Chapter 8

Joshua sat back on the chartered plane. It was an overnight flight, quiet, less scrutiny and time to think. He'd dated - if you could call a few nights in a hotel room a date - more than a few flight attendants over the years and his presence usually brought more than necessary attention.

The dinner with his father had unnerved him. He'd attended more from obligation than desire. He'd needed his father's help and hated that but finding Valerie was more important. He knew that and didn't hesitate but even so, between that and the farm incident, as he thought of long buried memories dredged up, followed by his enormous relief at seeing for himself she was safe and almost back to normal which meant generally pissed off, left him feeling destabilized. In his line of work that could be fatal.

After boarding school his father had insisted he follow his path to Oxford preferably to study world politics as it related to business, specifically Daine Investments, LLC. Still angry and feeling rebellious that became the last thing he wanted to do. He held dual British and American passports; his mother was American and for her they lived in New York. When she died his father began to groom his son as heir apparent without checking to see if that's what he wanted. And so from then on he wanted the opposite. The day he turned eighteen he'd enlisted in the U.S. Army, found basic training easier than navigating an elite British public school and was soon assigned to the famed Delta Squad.

Whether from talent, resentment or structure he'd thrived in the military. His commanders called him a natural. He could have made a fine career of it, risen through the ranks, possibly joint chief's one day but having made his point, after three years he was recruited into the C.I.A.. And more than anything in his entire life, pretending to be someone else, moving easily in different cultures, a facility with languages and a sense of who was lying, he became their top field agent. When, after five years and a legendary reputation, they'd assigned him a partner for a seemingly simple intel gathering he was miffed.

He didn't want or need a partner, they consistently lagged, asked too many questions or worse, thought it was some version of a TV buddy cop movie. He'd dispatched them all easily but this time he was given no choice. She was the new star on the horizon and had the expertise needed. He wasn't sure what he'd hated more, that she was female and considered his equal or that, grudgingly, he soon realized she was up to the job. He'd learned to respect her competence and if not her advice at least her insight into things he might have missed. If he'd harbored any personal feelings he kept them well hidden. Not like she came on to him; in fact generally she'd treated him as a necessary intrusion.

Lately, though, she'd been in his thoughts. Separated from her, not knowing if she was alive or where, had nearly destroyed him. His warning from Maya and escape from the farm in the nick of time had in fact almost gotten him caught when he broke cover to find her. If not for his father's available capital he might still be searching, incarcerated or dead. Even so, it hadn't been easy to trace her, she was under lockdown, hidden in plain sight but few willing to speak.

Once he'd found her he needed to know how they had been compromised or at least who had screwed up, how they'd been located and why she'd been so easily released. Nothing made much sense. But she was safe and that was really all that mattered to him right now. Probably not happy that he was off without her but she'd get over that. His father, too, wanted what all aging fathers want, peace with their son. But did his son want that? Joshua was not sure.

He also had decidedly mixed feelings about the plan to rescue Lina and bring her to their home. It was doable, he thought, but felt a piece was missing. Like why now? He knew his father owed Yevi a great deal and Joshua never knew what that was and not sure he cared. He was never as enamored of him and while there had been attempts to put him and Lina together, he'd made sure it never took. He didn't think she much liked him either, her tastes ran to the Daine lifestyle not the one he lived. If he used one word for her it would be predatory. He didn't think she was evil just a woman enamored of the good life. He'd been born to it and as such, it never mattered. As someone once said, only the well off say money isn't important to happiness.

All those thoughts continued to swirl in him when suddenly, not to his liking, popped in Doctor Cheng. The more he tried to shut it down the more dominant what she'd told him became. He suspected she was right about finding an outlet for his emerging emotions but early on he'd vowed never to need anyone again and he'd done just fine.

Or had he? Would he have been the same success or even still been alive were he not Bennett Daine's son? As to Valerie, he'd rarely confided in her and never about his personal life but he had often sensed she knew more than he knew about himself. He knew her background, of course, full dossier. She'd never spoken of that either, her life as disrupted as his. Is that why they made a great team, each kept their secrets inside?

The rhythm of the plane and emotional overload overtook him and he drifted into sleep.

#   #

Shortly after sunrise, the plane banked to land at Skavsta Airport's far runway privately owned, where his presence would hopefully go unnoticed. It was an hour's drive into Stockholm but that would give him time to forge a plan. He grabbed his gear, thanked the crew and hurried through the V.I.P. customs setup. Stockholm was not a city he knew well but had given thought to living on one of Sweden's hundreds of habitable islands, away from, what? He wasn't sure what stopped him, he had the resources, he'd put in his time at the Company. Whatever was going on inside him, he wasn't ready to be put out to pasture or, during winter, an ice floe. Something felt too permanent about that thought. Maybe after this job he would take some time and think through his future. He'd never done that, everything was a reaction to doing the opposite of expectations; maybe now it was time to figure out what he wanted without outside interference.

He picked up the ordered car and headed out. He'd scoured a map of Stockholm on the plane. He rarely used G.P.S., it could be unreliable. For this job he'd be off the grid. He'd often worked without backup and he couldn't yet say why he was bothered about this venture. There were no obvious red flags other than some seriously watchful eyes that would be on Lina. He wasn't sure she knew what was coming or even if she wanted to be whisked off. He hadn't talked to her in years; he knew she was married and had a lavish life in Moscow but she'd have the same standard of living in America. He hoped Yevi wasn't making the decision for her. He was going in blind and he didn't like that.

He pulled up to the Berns Hotel, a high end boutique establishment that understood privacy, not far from *Gamla Stan* or Old Town and edging a park for quick getaways. His cover was his least favorite, his father's son, the playboy. He'd used it over the years as Valerie had used her background but ironically it was the only time he felt like a fraud. It wasn't who he was, he told himself even as he knew its value. Again, Doctor Cheng's words came back. He hadn't had a blackout since the cabin but he knew the problem was not resolved; the suddenness worried him more than the memories.

Time to get to work, thoughts would have to wait. He had three days to suss out what he could The first thing he needed to do was work out a timeline; to know where everyone would be and why. Anyone out of sequence would be suspect. .He couldn't go through regular channels; whatever this was it wasn't sanctioned.

Johannes Skölvig, a contact from the old days who likely had kept his hand in and could help with logistics, would be in his 80s now and hopefully still alive. He was a wily old coot even then but for the right price, willing to share. He sold to both sides, any side for that matter, it was all about the money for him. As such he could be trusted since bad info was bad for business. Somehow that simplicity appealed to Joshua and he had liked him.

An hour later in a roomy apartment in the *Norrmalm* area just north of the city proper or *Innerstaden*, he found Johannes, grayer of hair, slower but still spry with few signs of wear.

"So Joshua, how long has it been?"

"Montenegro, twelve years ago. You had a nice side business selling secrets to both sides during the Soviet *perestroika*."

He laughed heartily. "Those were wonderful days. No one knew anything and paid dearly for any news. And you must admit, my news was better than most."

"You always did have the contacts. Must be your Swedish charm." He took the offered *akvavit*.

"And that, my friend, is no doubt what you have come to see me about."

"It is. There is to be a talk at the upcoming Global Environmental Responsibility Forum gathering, about climate change and political policy with action plans to come out of it."

"Ah, yes, I have heard it may not be such a polite gathering. Many radical groups are forming. There is talk of moving it from the old Riksdag Building in town to

University to accommodate all. Better security in the Riksdag, any trouble can just toss in in the river but I guess they don't care if the school gets trashed. Some of these so-called planet lovers can be vicious in their demands." He laughed at his politically incorrect humor.

"And you can get me the blueprints?"

"You have only to ask."

"And pay?"

"I give you the friends and family rate."

Joshua laughed. "Is that more or less than your regular rate?"

He headed out with a handshake and decided to take a walking tour of the *Strandvägen* along the waterfront. Sweden was a series of islands forming archipelagos, surrounded by water, a long thin country, home to ten million people. The air was crisp and fresh, maybe he should return to the hotel for running shoes, it was a perfect day to blow out cobwebs and re-calibrate from his slide into too much that was personal. As he turned back towards the hotel he glanced at a message board with posters of events.

Suddenly he couldn't breathe. He looked around, could find nothing else that triggered his light headed feeling. A empty bench was near and he sat, frightened as to what was happening to him. Post traumatic stress came to mind but his military service was long past and it seemed unlikely. Was his father right? Time draws down no matter the resistance?

A few women pushing strollers looked at him curiously and walked on, a little faster. Finally he got up and rode a bus back to the hotel where he spent an hour in their workout room, forcing extraneous thoughts out of his mind. He'd been to Stockholm a few times over the years, to meet contacts or change flights, without incident although this was his first experience working there.

Which made him wonder about the assignment. Sure, his father and Yevi were friends and he knew Lina but this was extraction. Valerie was more familiar with the city, she'd used it as a secondary base prior to working with him, knew the language he thought. Yet when he'd suggested it his father had said Yevi wanted it done quietly and quickly. Lina would go with him, no questions asked. But to Joshua the more he thought about it the less it made sense. Before he could move forward though he had to know what was triggering his episodes. He decided to return to where it happened, to see if he could find the source.

At the same spot where he had stood before he looked around, studying everything within his sight line carefully. He walked to the message board. Finally his eyes settled on a poster for the Toy Museum and again, he started to get light-headed. He forced himself to focus. What was in that poster? He checked directions, not far at all, and ran the short distance.

At the entrance another flashback started. He quickly found a bench, out of sight from kids reluctantly being herded out as it neared closing. He let himself fall into his vision, of a boy with a woman, the boy excited to be seeing trains, roomfuls of trains, the woman laughing and saying, don't run, we have all day. But his father had said no, he couldn't waste time, he was coming to the bank with him where he would learn how to open an account in a foreign city. Looking at toy trains wasn't on the list. He remembered yelling at his father that when he took over they would be; he would buy all the trains in the world!

His mother had stood up for him. "Bennett, really, you must realize he's a boy and it's his birthday. We're going to the train museum as a birthday present. It's decided."

He was jumping with excitement. His father was frowning, displeased, but chose not to contradict his wife. She kissed him and said, "Don't fret, Bennett, a boy is entitled to a good time on his birthday. Didn't I show you a good time on your birthday?"

Bennett laughed. Joshua thought of it now as the first time he could recall his father laughing and in fact, he wasn't sure he remembered another time. Two years later his mother lay dying and neither had laughed much after that.

Joshua continued sitting, basking in the memory of his mother. Grief had buried so many thoughts but now he remembered her sunny disposition, her profound love of her son and husband. How different their lives would have been had she lived. As much as when he was ten, he felt her loss.

An elderly man in a well worn cardigan but with a strong step exited the museum and came over to sit next to him on the bench. He pulled out his pipe and lit it. He looked over.

"You came here as a boy, yes?"

Joshua hesitated but decided the man only wanted company. "Yes. My mother brought me. On my tenth birthday. I saw the poster and something clicked into my memory but it doesn't look familiar now."

The man smiled knowingly. "I hear that often. It is a small museum, our *Leksaksmuseet*, privately funded, part of the Tido Castle Collection. It used to be in *Mariatorget*, that's why it's different to you. But that place was too small and so we are here now. I cannot count the thousands of children who enter with excitement but leave with frowns at not being allowed to stay forever." The old man laughed; his teeth were yellowed but still intact.

"Do you work here?"

"My father was the caretaker and I suppose I grew up feeling all these toys were mine and I was to share them with others. I went off to a government job but returned with the children of my friends. My wife died in childbirth and I could never find another woman to love." He paused. "I apologize. One should not share so much to a stranger enjoying our beautiful weather today."

"I don't mind. My mother died a few years after we came here. Sometimes I have a hard time remembering her and sitting here has brought back a happy memory."

"Then come, I have just closed up but I can give you a private tour. Take all the time you want. When I retired I offered to help out for the owners. I find it makes me happy. What else would I do with my time, eh?"

Joshua knew he should be working but he followed the man inside. The trains were not as he remembered, so much smaller and he had no memory at all of the other collections. But he felt close to his mother in a way he had not since her passing. A wave of peace came over him as if she had been watching him all along for that moment. He did not believe in an afterlife but now he understood why many did. As he left he placed a generous donation into the box and thanked the man, named Gunnar, for helping him recreate his feelings as a boy.

"It's something that does not come easy."

"No. I can see that in you. You have a strong presence and must put out of mind that which interferes with your destiny."

"Destiny?"

"We all have a path that is chosen for us. We may not know it at the time but it appears. Some choose to ignore it but at their peril, I believe."

"Maybe now I will not ignore it. Thank you for your time."

"You are most welcome. And you may return at any time. What is that Shakespeare line, we are the stuff dreams are made of?"

"From *The Tempest*, yes."

"Remember. *Det är aldrig för sent*, it is never too late."

He shook the man's hand. "*Hejdå.*"

Daine returned to the hotel. He'd find out later why they'd been here, in Stockholm. Maybe his father's business, his mother was blond and pretty, maybe her parents were Swedish. His father had never told him how they'd met or where she'd grown up. Any topic that included her was off limits. But when this was over, he would have that talk with his father, about everything that went unsaid about his mother.

No time for reflection now, he had work to do. He wanted to know every inch of the *Riksdag* building, the old Swedish parliament building, on *Ridddarholmen*. He wished he could connect with Lina beforehand but she would be well guarded and not worth the risk. He just hoped his information was correct, that she was aware of the plan and would be no trouble. Unfortunately his few dealings with her made him suspect. Lina, even as a child, had never been trouble free. She was manipulative about getting her own way. She'd wanted to marry him and took it badly when rebuffed. She'd wanted his father's money not his love. When he'd suggested she marry his father she simply glared and walked out; they hadn't spoken since. And yet, here he was. Well, often he'd had much less than two days to prepare, time to get to work. But just in case, he'd bring Valerie in the loop. He'd left her with a burner phone; they were still partners and she would not take kindly to being completely left behind.

Maybe afterward, he'd be able to share these incidents. She had a point, he really had kept his thoughts at a distance. He'd told himself getting too involved would affect their work.

Suddenly he missed her. Not her assistance or her ability to maneuver but her. He wondered if she might be able to help sort why his nerves were on edge. Not the assignment, pretty straightforward, but something else, just out of reach. He used a public phone to call her. She would know how to hide the phone but in case, his message was cryptic and his voice accented on a different pitch.

"Hi Sweetie. I have to stay a few more days. Uncle Bernie's funeral planning is not going well, his blue blazer didn't fit and his children are in a snit, no idea why I'm here, not really close to the family. I should have brought you, you were right, as always, but no time to paint the town yellow. If I have to stay longer you can join me, there seems to be some confusion as to who's in charge but I'm sure I'll sort it out and be back soon."

It would put her on alert, easy to figure out the hotel, and using the flag colors for Sweden she would know where. The next step was to grab a fistful of *kronor* for Johannes and pick up the blueprints. But when he got there, the man was hesitant.

"What's wrong?"

"I wish I could tell you. Usually I can get my needs without trouble, I know many people. This time they were afraid. Someone is worried about that gathering and checking everything. There are rumors of an outside group coming in to cause trouble. No one knows why, there have been many climate conferences in Stockholm, we are a leader in climate protection."

"I know. That's why the city was chosen. I'm not concerned with that. I'm sure it's something that doesn't concern me but I will be watchful. Thank you."

"I had to pay extra for these, because of the fears."

"Have I ever not met your price?"

"You have always been my favorite to do business with. You understand a man's expenses."

"If you hear more, let me know. In case it overlaps I'd like to be prepared. And whatever the other side pays I will double it but only if I'm the only one. Don't play both sides with me. This time it will be too risky for you."

Johannes nodded solemnly. He knew his dangers very well.

Joshua returned to the hotel and studied the prints thoroughly, until he'd memorized every inch. He also knew that buildings could be updated but blueprints not so carefully. He would have preferred to make a tour, preferably after hours, in and out, silently but with all the new digital and imaging equipment available it was almost impossible to avoid a video capture. So far he believed he was unnoticed but that could change fast if he wasn't careful.

His presence in Stockholm while Yevi gave a speech, family friend or not, might set off alarms in the wrong places. He wanted to see for himself the level of security. It was Sweden; they were familiar with large scale events and more than competent with crowds but maybe not always prepared for the worst. He pondered a rooftop entrance but on an island the potential of too many visible windows and stargazing with a wandering telescope, hiding in plain sight would have to do. He would have to suss out what he could.

He stopped at the business center to put the blueprints through the shredder then went to the front desk to leave a message for Valerie, as a precaution. Then he checked out, being in one place too long is more likely to be noticed.

He would pick up a guide book and head for an ale house, playing the eco-tourist come to join the resistance. A few beers in and someone was always willing to share the latest gossip.

# #

Chapter 9

Derek Applegate sat, slouched and still a little light headed. He couldn't decide if he were worried or having a good time. They'd brought him water and some crackers from the vending machine. Now he wasn't sure if he should leave the crumbs on the table or swish off to the floor.

He'd faced down Feds before, as a teenaged hacker he'd gotten carried away, more interested with how deep he could troll than with consequences. As a result he wasn't as cautious as he soon realized he should have been.

When the Feds had knocked on his door he'd been busy in his room but his mother's screech, there was no other word for it, brought him down. Two men in suits and two behind in SWAT gear looked at him, surprised. He hadn't yet had his growth spurt and so appeared even younger than he was. His lawyer demanded a jury trial. The prosecution, from experience, knew that few on the jury would convict someone who looked like their grandson for "playing around" on his computer. As a result they offered a plea deal to work for the government as ten years probation, record clean. A generous offer for breaking into government security, they'd told her. It seemed a lifetime to him but his mother didn't hesitate, she had instantly agreed. Her look said that was final and he was still young enough that his mother's authority was far more convincing than the actual law.

He was allowed to finish high school, computer use monitored, then a year of training - like he needed that, he had groused every day to no one who cared - and had been assigned to tracking money. Boring. Worse, he'd be nearly thirty before released, old age before even getting started. His fellow employees treated him like a punk kid at best, dangerous at worst. Life was bleak.

Until Valerie arrived, as unhappy to be there as he was. She was his kindred spirit even if they had never spoken; she'd barely acknowledged his existence but then, she ignored everyone. He was pretty sure he was going to marry her.

So facing down two agents, one an arrogant male who thought he could intimidate him because of his youth and a female, trying to appear motherly and his friend when she was at least forty, did not phase him. Besides, they hadn't called his mother. He could handle this.

Valerie, the only person who mattered to him right now, had sent him her files on Missy's hidden funds; well to be precise he'd hacked into her computer to read them. She hadn't really shut down properly before heading to Missy's office but he was sure she meant to send them. But how much to tell these two agents? He wanted to protect her as much as possible and didn't want to go to jail.

"Tell us again what you saw." The woman spoke, he'd missed her name when introduced. He would have preferred the man as women in authority still unnerved him.

"I saw Missy order her into the office. In twenty minutes or so they left. I could tell by Valerie's expression something was wrong so I thought maybe I should follow, in case... um, well, Valerie had unearthed an offshore account of Missy's, and she might want to, um, do her harm."

"What offshore account would that be?"

Uh oh. "I'm not sure. She was telling me about it when Missy interrupted. She was mad."

"Why was she mad?"

He shrugged. "She just said, my office. Now. Like that. But it must've been about her hidden money. Although it wasn't really well hidden so maybe it wasn't secret, an inheritance or something, to avoid taxes." Their expressions didn't change. "She closed the curtains and then after a while they left."

"And you followed."

"Well, not at first. I was going to the bathroom and saw them go into the stairwell. That seemed strange."

"Why did it seem strange?"

"Dunno, just did."

"Did you run or walk down the stairwell?"

"Huh? I dunno, it's a stairwell. I heard them and waited until the outside door closed."

"So you went down the stairwell after they exited?"

"I guess."

"What were they doing when you arrived on the scene?"

Trick question. "Nothing."

"Nothing?" The man broke in and scoffed. That irritated Derek.

"I told you, Missy was angry. She had a gun." He was pretty sure she had one, why else would Valerie leave with her, although maybe he shouldn't sound so sure.

"Did you see who fired the shot?"

"Yes. No. Well, not exactly. But it was from further off, I'm positive of that, but I didn't see from where exactly," or at all if he were strictly honest but he was positive Valerie was innocent, so it must have been like that. "I'm sure Missy meant to harm Valerie, you could see it in her eyes."

"You were close enough to see her eyes?" The man looked like he wanted to squish him like a bug.

"Uh, more of a feeling, then, uh, some guys came. With guns."

"And you fainted." The man was not as good looking as he seemed to think and was trying to rile him.

"I don't like guns."

They watched him no doubt thinking the silence would unnerve him but he was used to ignoring adults. He returned their blank stares.

"Thank you for your help. Someone will be in with your statement to sign."

The two stood up and walked out without another glance at him, leaving him sitting there wondering where Valerie was and when he could get to his computer in case she tried to contact him. But she was safe, they hadn't caught her, that much was clear. For that, he was pleased.

He brushed the crumbs onto the floor.

#   #

Valerie was on the run, she knew they'd be looking for her. A dead assistant deputy director was not something to leave and rush off. But they'd spend hours sorting it out while she explained about the hidden account and Missy having no idea. She had to get to Joshua, to warn him that someone wanted him neutralized. Who and why were a mystery but maybe he'd know, he'd hinted as much. She'd remind him he had a partner, no more secrets.

And now, likely already on his way to, right, Stockholm, to protect a friend of his father's. Some big speech that was sure to set off alarms, he'd said. How did that factor in?

She'd lost the shooter, he had distance and a prepared exit. Which opened up a question as to how he knew they'd be there and more confusing, why kill Missy? Someone had used her in their plans, but why? Why use her only to shoot her in plain sight? A planned assassination or a panic attack to shut her up, which seemed likely as she was about to confess who was behind her actions. Even so, it didn't make sense.

She could trace it through the last phone call but she didn't have time for that now. She couldn't return to her car or her apartment and an alert would go out for public transportation soon enough. She had to get to Stockholm but first she needed a fake I.D. and money.

Her phone was in her purse locked in her desk. Just as well, they'd have a trace on it by now. The prepaid phone Joshua gave her was buried under her brother's headstone, Christian Jay Rhodes, age 28. It was fake like everything else in her life. Chris had been cremated, at least the prosecution had allocated funds for that. Her mother had picked up the ashes then, hysterical, had thrown them against the wall the day the movers came, one hurt too many. Valerie, furious that her mother had been too "depressed" to organize a memorial since none of his so called friends were willing to be tainted with the family shame. As soon as she had enough money she bought a proper headstone near the training facility so she could tell him about her new job and that she'd be gone a while. When she had returned stateside, out of habit she began to hide fake I.D.'s and currencies along with an unregistered gun; it gave her an excuse to visit and talk to him about her new situation. She had no one else to confide in and missed him so much. So when that person Rod told her to hide the phone she knew no one would think to look for it there.

At the end of the block an Uber driver let out a fare. She rushed over and offered cash, which she always stuck in her bra as backup usually for the gun range so as to not use a traceable credit card. The driver was certainly amenable to off the book money.

She had him stop a few blocks away. He'd clocked her face but unlikely she'd be on the evening news. She'd be long gone in any event. Checking to be sure no one was around she easily dug out the phone and the computer stick she'd nearly forgotten about along with the fake I.D. she had made when barred from travel after her mandatory reassignment, some cash and a charger. It was several hours to sundown and she couldn't take a chance to wander so she hunched down against the headstone wishing that she could go back in time. Their last conversation had been an argument. She'd gotten engaged in college, to someone Chris deemed unworthy and he had argued against the match. He turned out to be right, her fiance had dumped her before the ink on the subpoena was dry. He'd been such a great older brother but after her father was arrested he crawled inside himself, refused to talk. She'd never learned if he suspected.

As everyone left the cemetery's small office complex she headed up to break in, charge the phone and call for a ride when she noticed one car remained in the lot. No lights were on inside; she waited a while longer to be sure but it appeared to be a company car, for errands maybe. Did it run? Again, luck was with her, the car was old enough to be easily hot wired.

She was careful to leave no fingerprints, DNA took longer to process, and left it several miles from the cabin in a Walmart parking lot, eyed by a few homeless she hoped had less interest in her description. She'd run the rest of the way, her forced walk had given her a scope of the area. Already a day was wasted and no doubt they were honing in on everywhere she'd ever been. Hopefully the Daine cabin was off their grid and security as tight as he'd said.

At the cabin, nearing midnight she banged on the front door. In less than sixty seconds two armed men were behind her.

"Joshua Daine. I need to speak to Joshua." She was still catching her breath, hands up, against the flashlight beam, when one of the men handed her his phone.

"Bernmeister. This better be good."

# #

Professor Yevgeny Yurovinsky was restless. The trip from Oxford to Stockholm the day before had been uneventful. A private plane had flown him and his minders but as holder of an E.U. passport he didn't need to go through customs. They did, however, and Olaf and his friends had whisked him away and into what he presumed was a safe harbor hotel. They would be frantically searching for him but for now, he hoped, he would have some time to do what he needed to prepare. They could not be obvious about hunting for him and would in any event know where he'd be in two days. He certainly wouldn't report their failure and he doubted they would. They would report all was well, he was safely tucked up. Which was true, they just didn't know where. But they'd manage, they were no doubt experts at self protection or they would not have been allowed out of Russia to be his caretakers. Still, he had to be mindful of them; he was sure they could do harm if pushed.

He was more nervous about his upcoming speech. So much riding on it and he could not possibly know the outcome. He had not heard from his daughter in too long. That frightened him. This was all arranged to bring her to safety, if he couldn't do that nothing else mattered. He trusted his friend Bennett to do his part but without knowing his plans he was not able to concentrate. This speech mattered to the world. Leaders who chose power and wealth over people were destroying the planet. Children were getting involved, creating worldwide demonstrations, he had to give them a beacon. He had no grandchildren yet but he hoped

Lina, once safe in America, would give him that joy. Even if he did not live to see it he would know he had worked to make that as yet unborn person's world a better place. He had to succeed, so much at stake.

There was a knock at the door. Olaf or something, he had barely paid attention when told he would be under protection at all times and not to worry, they were the best. He knew the dangers and the presumed leader of those who met him, Olaf Langsston - right, that was the name - had assured him they had taken every precaution and then some. Frankly, he didn't look it, small and wiry, maybe one of those martial arts people. Right now, Yurovinsky couldn't think of that. He had to rehearse his speech, it had to be perfect so they couldn't discredit him. His speech would go viral, was that the right word? So much new technology, he tried to keep up but it kept changing. If only he had a grandchild to keep him current. And that brought his thoughts back to Lina, which set him off to worrying again.

He knew Stockholm fairly well, having come over for various conferences over the years but this was different. Or maybe he was just old, his faculties leaving him. Bennett had always been loyal, would he fail him now? No, he was sure of his friend, not because he owed his family so much. They shared a secret that no one knew, he was sure of that. Or was he? Secrets have a way of getting out over time. A word here, a glance there, old files opened for some reason. But he couldn't call him either, any contact to anyone except for the purpose he was here for could open dangerous doors.

He tried to concentrate on his speech. He'd given many before, but this would strike many as incendiary because he was challenging Russia and the U.S. for their indifference, propagating power over saving the planet. Greed had overtaken leaders and their followers, no thought to future generations. The rich can protect themselves they think, while those less fortunate are held back by short sighted and dangerous policies. Rebellions are a beginning, they will grow but those, while necessary, are not as productive as governments taking the lead.

"We must be vigilant. So I am today announcing a fellowship grant to all resisters, who stand in defiance of those who would do harm. The source for this is anonymous and will remain so but it will have but one goal, the survival of our planet and a return to morality. Leaders who resist beware, we are coming for you."

He hadn't realized he was speaking aloud when Olaf entered. "Bravo, excellent." He applauded lightly. "Excuse me, Doktor Yurovinsky, I do not mean to interrupt. There is someone to see you. He would not leave his name."

It must be Bennett. Instead he found a large Russian, an expression of hatred that he quickly disguised with a smile that didn't reach his eyes. Behind him was one of Olaf's men, taller and more muscular.

"Yes?"

The man silently handed him a piece of paper. Then, without a word he left. Yurovinsky opened the note. It was from Lina, instantly he relaxed. It read: "My darling Papa, I cannot wait to hear your speech, and to see you after so long. I will be the one clapping the loudest for your success. Love from all my heart, Lina."

He broke into a smile and told Olaf not to disturb him, he would be in his room working on his speech.

Olaf nodded and when the adjoining door closed, picked up his phone to make a call. When answered, he said, "It's all set. *Allt är bra.*"

#   #

Bennett Daine, too, was feeling restless. He was in New York, preparing to walk one of his companion's daughters down the aisle. Her father was dead and while he barely knew the girls he knew it was expected of him as her mother's… what's the term? Significant other? Mistress? Consort? Sex partner? Arm candy? If he were honest he had to admit he rarely thought about Cortina D'Angelo, society matron and widow. His presence as a wealthy bachelor at events always brought out all the sisters, nieces, daughters, even married women looking to move up, sought after for the ride he could give them. Corie had her own money, three daughters she adored, no need to remarry and a vibrant social and volunteer life. She demanded little of him and each only needed a social and bed partner. The result was, to his mind, a perfect relationship. But when her brother had suffered a mild heart attack and couldn't travel he'd agreed to be the stand-in father to walk Diedre, the oldest, down the aisle.

He'd had to cancel his appearance at Yevi's speech and had not been able to contact him with apologies. He knew his friend would understand, business often changed plans and he would leave for Stockholm as soon as he could, his plane was ready to go after his toast and dance with the bride and bride's mother. Joshua, he knew, would be there, a plan in place.

He'd made a hash of that relationship and he also knew time for fixing it was drawing down. But how to reach a man who'd spent his life running from everything his father had built? He wanted to drop everything and race to Stockholm, talk to him, but it would only make it worse. Joshua knew his job, he'd done extractions many times. And of course that was what worried Daine, his son was well known in the wrong circles and living on the edge was increasingly more dangerous. His unease, he hoped, was unwarranted.

Corie walked in with a flower for his suit, a gathering of the clan dinner, the tux would come tomorrow. She was a confident well put together woman, attractive in her own right and enhanced by wealth. Salon streaked blond hair today piled on her head for the occasion, golden complexion from her regular facials and perfect nails in a neutral color. She wore a beige silk suit with a midnight blue silk shirt with only a simple gold chain and cross she cherished, always worn, given by her husband from his beloved grandmother on their wedding day.

She kissed Bennett lightly on the cheek and put the orchid in his lapel and fussed a bit over his suit, straightened his tie, less because he needed it than she needed to do something with her hands. She wore no rings as she believed that anything other than a gold band was ostentatious. Carlos and Bennett had been acquaintances and before his wife died, often saw each other at functions. When Carlos died he came to the funeral and she learned he had authorized Bennett to handle the financial side of her life. She was grateful and quickly realized he needed someone by his side. It served them both well.

"I know this is not your favorite thing, Bennett. Daughters require so much more care than a son. I wish he were here, no, not to push onto the other two but you would be much happier, no?"

He smiled. "Yes. But I'm not sure about daughters needing more. I have a lot to make up to him. He never seemed to want my help, though."

"Of course not. You are a powerful man. He needed to make his own way to feel he is his own man. One day he will return, mark my words. When he can meet you as an equal. But a daughter? You would hate all the men she liked but she would remain yours forever. No so with mothers and daughters."

"Why do they not tell you how hard it is to be a parent?"

She laughed. "They do. We just don't listen. Now come, it's almost time to meet the groom's extended family before the big event. And Bennett, thank you. I could not have done this alone. You are a true friend." She laughed again. "And so much more."

He looked at her, thinking she had been a beacon for him, also. Never demanding, always supportive, was he so callous as to take all that for granted? Why had he never realized that before?

# #

Joshua was standing near the edge of a small group touring the old parliamentary building, now a museum of sorts. It was used for various events to pay for maintenance and upkeep since it had a history that made tearing it down a political minefield. He wore glasses and a plaid shirt with khaki pants and light jacket; in his hand was a well worn guidebook. He stood close enough to a woman with two children that it appeared they were together. However, had anyone thought to notice, neither ever looked at the other.

Joshua was looking for something specific and when they rounded a corner heading for a staircase he saw the person he wanted, a tall security guard, going into the restroom behind the staircase. As his fellow tourists kept their eyes on the stairs going up he peeled off to the side and into the same restroom. Inside he tossed the guidebook into the trash, checked that no other person was in there and stuck a broom handle through the door to block it.

The man finished and at the washbasin Joshua stuck a gun in his back. The man started to turn and was put in a headlock. "I'm not going to hurt you. I just need a favor."

As his neck was twisted precariously he could only nod an inch. He fought to not act as scared as he was, two months into the job he was only trained to spot thieves. He wasn't sure what to do.

"I'm going to let go but if you move I'll break your arm."

Again, the man tried to nod, rubbing his neck when Joshua let go.

Joshua pulled out a large wad of cash and held it up. "This is yours. I want you to call in sick for a couple of days and change clothes with me. I'm not going to blow anything up and you can return in a few days, richer and deny knowing anything. Your uniform was stolen. Do you understand?"

He nodded, reaching for the money. Joshua held it back. "Your clothes first. Oh, and if you say anything I will break both arms."

The man's eyes widened. He went into a stall to remove his uniform. Joshua removed his jacket and unbuttoned his shirt, tossing his glasses into the trash.

# #

Lars-Villig Birkstraach, the man in charge of the Global Environmental Responsibility Forum, stood on the empty stage looking out over the meeting hall. Today it was empty but tomorrow would be filled with those wanting change and possibly some who did not. That did not always make for a peaceful mix. He was not a man who worried excessively nor did he appear pleased as his long efforts were about to come to fruition. He'd heard the rumors of outside interference and he knew the risks.

He'd been a lifelong diplomat, well connected, socially adept, highly intelligent and well spoken in several languages. He'd been witness to many historical events, knew world leaders by their first name, most of whom were gone now, replaced by less disciplined and more narrow thinkers. He had seen many unfortunate events and was more than ready to move away, had hoped for a blissful retirement with his devoted Hilda on a government pension. Until their beloved granddaughter had died of a rare poison ingested from a substance that should have been banned except for lobbying by the chemical company that made it. From that moment on he had one purpose, to hold those who put profit over children to be held accountable.

As he began his quest he learned how deep and pervasive was the problem. Grief turned to anger turned to activism.

He would not fail in this mission.

#   #

Chapter 10

Birkstraach, after much deliberation, had decided the Global Environmental Responsibility Forum was to be held in *Gamla Riksdagshuse*t, the Old Parliament Building in central Stockholm. Parliament had moved over a century ago to a newer building on nearby *Helgeandsholmen*, both on small islands within the district *Gamla Stan* or Old Town. The rectangular red brick building had over the years served many purposes but was eventually overhauled with energy efficiency and stood proud again. It's seating was somewhat limited, around four hundred which to Berkstraach seemed the right number. Also, Parliamentarian offices would not be disturbed and tours could be shut down for the day. As it was accessible by *Riddarholsbron* or bridge it was deemed more manageable. Protesters could be kept across the *Riddarfjärden* to lessen their impact during the event.

The meeting chamber with its layers of seating so all would have a good view, acoustics better than most opera houses, was beginning to fill up. First in were the cameras, it would all be filmed and presented live in many areas around the world. Climate change and the accompanying destruction of the planet had finally, perhaps due to the efforts of children and new scientific reports not to mention weather disruption was now of concern to many. It had always hovered in the background, diehard environmentalists led the charge but not all listened. Corporations and marketing had made it too easy to ignore in one's daily life. Opposition was smart and took a longer view, get into power to undo regulations and change the narrative. Find a fear factor to bring voters into line. Voters who feared for their livelihood would vote for those who demonized a culprit; fear removed logic. Outsourcing killed many a town and village but if the propaganda machine can make it seem that it was immigrants taking away jobs or discarding values, code for "not us," nothing else was scrutinized.

And so it began, the loosening of any regulation that interfered with profits and that was most of them that protected people. Stuff the courts with conservative judges who didn't automatically rule for the environment. Throw enough money around that politicians didn't dare stand up for what was right. Never mind constituents, it was large donors that mattered at election time. Be sure each elected official knew that what comes in can go to an opponent just as fast. Make sure the ones who do your bidding are well cared for, their family with jobs or luxury vacations. For some, it became a very short step from honor to greed to acceptance.

#   #

The buzz was beginning. Seats in front were assigned but in the higher, back reaches it was first come first served. All were searched not just for weapons but for provocative signs, even marking pens were confiscated. Cell phones turned off, any found turned on inside would be taken. The organizers expected trouble. They knew protesters, some possibly hired to disrupt, would line the building and the banks of the river outside so that comings and goings would be forced to hear and see their signs and chants. That was their right but inside the tight quarters they could better control the mob. Rumors were circulated about moving the event to the University in hopes that some protesters would go there instead.

A podium was set up, microphones tested, side chairs brought out with bottles of water on the little tables. There would be an introduction of a moderator who would begin a panel discussion with a token opposition view although she had been carefully chosen as a firebrand who would be booed often, thereby negating her views. The four other panelists were experts in different fields: *economics of alternate energy, biological diversity and perils of massive extinction, timeline for reversing destruction, ocean cleanup and pesticides as murder for profit.* An action plan would be disseminated containing immediate and long term regulations needed along with how to organize and lobby political leaders. Birkstraach was thorough. He knew he could not continue forever so he would bring together groups that previously had resisted sharing their turf. He utilized diplomacy skills learned over decades. The event would be his legacy.

The theme of the conference was "*We cannot fight for our planet when we are fighting each other.*" Everyone in the room had pledged to return to their countries and begin the process. No longer would it be separated groups, all doing good work but limited by locale and numbers. No, this conference was about bringing all groups into one tent. They could of course continue their own course but without total commitment as a whole they would fail. The fight for money was ongoing and if they coordinated that would stretch their budgets. Infighting, especially when the opposition spread rumors, was detrimental and effective. They would not let that happen; they would unite as one. The planet, the future, the very existence of life was at stake.

Yevgeny Yurovinsky's speech would end the conference. His radical views were well known among the elite but this was the first time he would become a global household name. His speech would be the lightning rod that began the movement. A Russian dissident who challenged the system and won. It would be huge. Already two movies on his life were in the works, numerous books would be released and the children of the movement would grow up and become the future leaders the planet so desperately needed.

Lars-Villig Birkstraach watched over everything from the rafters. He had not seen Yurovinsky's speech beforehand and that, in a dissident, was worrisome.

He checked his watch. It was almost time.

#   #

Birkstraach entered the stage to the podium as the room continued to applaud the panel discussion, now exiting to expectant cheers. He waited for the noise to lessen and began his prepared speech into the microphone.

"And now, gathered guests, we are all grateful for their input to our cause. There are prepared handouts for all who wish to join our action plan. Remember that our theme today is we can't fight global warming and climate change if we're fighting each other. We know there are many differences among us but we must come together on the basic solutions and to further this issue onto the world."

He paused for a few cheers and "right on's."

"To that end we have a brilliant scientist who will bring his expertise to our gathering. He is, as many of you are aware, a man who has run from tyranny and brought his knowledge so that all can share and learn. A man now a tutor at Oxford University, at St. Catherine's College, in residence and, may I add, a friend to me as well as to all of us. Please welcome Doktor Yevgeny Yurovinsky."

To thunderous applause and cheers, the keynote speaker they have waited for strode confidently onto the stage. Some had heard rumors he was going to take on the establishment and they had tried to silence him; some had worried he would be stopped. The crowd roared as the keynote speaker stepped to the podium. Wearing a coat and tie, his hair combed for the event, he and Birkstraach shook hands, then embraced. He looked out upon the gathering as the cheers grow louder, put his hands up as he waited for the silence but didn't attempt to rush. Birkstraach stepped to the side, still apprehensive but hopeful. This could be their moment.

Lina, with her bodyguard who had brought the letter to her father, entered quietly from a side door and sat in the reserved seats in front. Some audience members noticed and an underlying buzz could be heard. She put her hand to her heart with a smile that expressed how happy she was to join her father on this momentous occasion. He visibly brightened.

"Thank you all for inviting me. It is a great honor for me to be here, to speak to a group so committed to saving our planet before it is too late. Not so many years ago I lived and worked in Russia where I was not allowed to speak of this. I tried to give warnings. Other scientists, too, we were all ignored or ostracized, sometimes even jailed. Yes, it is true. Truth tellers are a threat to those who want profit above all else. Yet Russia, full of beautiful people but despotic leaders, is a country rich in minerals and marine life and it could do much to lead the world." He paused for effect. "And yet, they do nothing." Again, he paused. "But it is not just my beloved boyhood home but the great power of the United States that has joined in doing nothing. They are failing us, our children and our grandchildren. Other countries will join them to limit positive change, afraid of being shut out by those that rule with unbridled power."

He began pacing, his voice growing more passionate. "It is greed that drives them and they bring fear to all that challenge them. We cannot let them. This planet has already begun it's slide to the abyss. Floods and hurricanes followed by drought and fires. Mother Nature, she is very mad at us, we have destroyed her faith in humanity."

He stared down into the audience. "No! We still have time. We have time to limit fossil fuels, to tell giant oil corporations they do not own us and bring down the politicians they do own. We have time to harness the great sun and wind, for good, not for higher and higher temperatures and tornadoes but to work our engines and light our homes. Technology can be our friend, it should not just be about making money but about innovation that will save us from annihilation."

He paused until all was silent. He reached into his pocket and pulled out a fistful of dollars, raised his hand high. "Green is the color of the environment and it is also the color of money, they belong together. Saving our planet can be profitable. But it will not be profitable to those who refuse to do what is right." He raised his other hand in a clasp.

Rousing cheers broke out, the room began to stand and cheer. From the wings, Birkstraach allowed himself a small smile.

More confident than before, as the room quieted he continued. "Unfortunately, the only interest of our leaders after years of repression and poverty was the oil reserves. Fortune to be handed out to a few who curried favor. We became a society of many who continued to struggle and the few who thrived. And Russia is not the only country where profit matters more than people. Many species vital to our very survival face extinction every day from our reliance on fossil fuels that created greenhouse gases. The most vulnerable will disappear first and be hardly noticed until it's too late. A balanced ecosystem is crucial to our ultimate survival. So why don't they listen?"

He paused as the crowd responded. "I will tell you why."

# #

Joshua, in the borrowed guard's uniform, half hidden in the shadows, moved down the side aisle, closer to his target. There were a half dozen other guards stationed around the room. They gave no notice of him but Olaf, offstage, noticed. He was in charge of all security and this was a new one to be watched. He knew one guard had called in sick but he had not authorized a replacement. He would fire whoever took it upon himself to do that. He looked back at the speaker in time to see Doktor Yurovinsky, who had also noticed the new guard, dip his head in an imperceptive nod. Olaf was now even more curious. Maybe he had brought his own security and chose not to tell him? For what purpose?

Yurovinsky continued, "Yes, I am speaking to the choir. You and I, we agree on the problem but we do not always agree on the solution. I caution you all, we must come together now so we can all go to our separate homes as one and become the next generation of activists. Are you with me?"

More cheers. This time he holds up his hand to quiet. "There is more. Before we can fight we must know whom we are fighting. I have brought a list of names, those against us, some will be of great surprise to you, some have ignored our pleas and are well known, but we must be vigilant." Expectant murmurs roll through the audience. He looked down at his daughter, nodding, as he pulled a sheet of paper from his pocket.

Lina looked up lovingly, a doting daughter. She put her fingers to her lips and blew him a tiny kiss.

Suddenly the lights went dark. A few screamed, a few shouted, "Hey, turn them back on," and above the din, two gunshots.

#   #

Chapter 11

Nigel Suffington had come early to scope out the venue. He had checked the exits and using one of his fake I.D.s that he kept in his lock box for his various free lance jobs he was allowed to wander freely. He wasn't pleased, too many alcoves and columns in which to hide. Security at the entrance was tight and the building was on an island but if someone got in, as he had, they could do some damage. That, however, wasn't his job. He'd been hired as an observer and backup should it be needed. His focus was the speaker, that he remain safe. He had found an aisle seat, on the side, for easy maneuverability. It also allowed him to stretch his bad leg into the aisle, welcome relief.

He was on disability and due to spartan living he could choose when and with whom he worked. No one knew he spent most days in pain from his wounds but other than a strict regimen of careful workouts and protein shakes he took nothing for it. If his life lacked anything he refused it entry into his thoughts.

Being a soldier was all he had ever wanted. A working class lad from Northern England, Little Lever to be exact, part of Bolton proper in Lancashire, a simple village of decent people. He'd never bothered elongating his vowels like some of his classmates; he was who he was. Except for sports, school was never of much interest. There was no money for a public school let alone his mediocre grades but thanks to his mother's love of reading he had toured the world in his mind. Until one day a neighbor returned home, in the spiffiest uniform he'd ever seen. From that moment his fate was sealed.

The first three years, in Afghanistan, were his happiest ever. His squad was tight, he'd showed the Americans how to play real football, which they insisted was called soccer; they taught him basketball and, at almost a head taller, he'd excelled. He trained hard, played hard and formed a tight bond that only men, and now women, did in war. He saw things he wished he hadn't but he'd always believed in the mission, that they could right the world by their presence and fighting skill. Long before cynicism had set in, however, the truck ahead in the convoy was hit by a bomb. As he and his fellow soldiers rushed to help their comrades he'd been hit by shrapnel from a second bomb. At the end of the day, all but six were killed and two wounded. He'd regained consciousness in a military hospital far removed from the fighting. His first words to the doctor were when could he return.

The wound, or more specifically the loss of his left leg below the knee, ushered him out of active duty. That realization came as a blow and not just literally. He'd spent a year hoping the nurses would leave him alone long enough to end it all. But he was good looking with smooth dark skin and mixed race features, his mother Indian, his father Jamaican and they fussed over him way more than his wounds warranted.

One day Rod Bernmeister had come through the ward. His boss, Bennett Daine, was holed up in an all day negotiation and he was free to roam the city until called. He preferred to stay close but Daine had insisted he leave, wander the city, they were well guarded at 10 Downing. One look and Rod knew they didn't like outsiders trying to do their job. Since he'd never give his boss reason to question his motives he decided to visit a veterans' hospital. He'd done that a few times in the States, on a rare day off. He knew he'd been lucky in battle but had seen too many friends die or sent home with missing parts. It was the least he could do and sometimes he could help.

That day, he struck up a conversation with Nigel. He might not know what the man was going through but he recognized his sense of loss. He'd been deployed so long his wife had found someone else. Loss was loss, be it a wife or a body part or a chosen career.

Bernmeister had smuggled in a pint of really good Scotch and they drank and talked. When he stood to leave he told Nigel he would be put on retainer when released from hospital. His boss had grown up in England and came back often. He needed reliable backup.

Nigel, renewed, accepted his new leg and put everything he had into physical therapy so that rarely could anyone tell by watching him walk. Only when tired did he allow a small limp.

Nigel owed everything to Rod Bernmeister and no matter the job he was eager. Not that sitting at an all day seminar on weather was his cup of tea, so to speak, but if Rod wanted him to babysit a Russian defector that was just fine with him.

Rod had told him that Mr. Daine's son would be there but he had another assignment. Only if he needed help should he be concerned. He'd never met him but one guard, partially hidden in shadow next to a wall column while the other guards trolled for open cell phones, fit the profile. He clocked him but for now not his concern. He continued to study the brochure, might be interesting after all.

When the two gunshots added further pandemonium and confusion to the darkened auditorium, Suffington was perhaps the only person still calm. First, he called Bernmeister. He'd seen Mr. Daine's son follow the professor's daughter through the same door they had arrived, into the lighted hallway.

He moved quickly through the terrified audience and slipped out a side door leading to the stage; his job was to stay with the professor.

When the lights returned some in the crowd began a rush to the exits, some had ducked below their seats. Yurovinsky was on the ground, a splotch of blood seeping into his coat from his abdomen. Olaf had rushed to him in the dark, nearly tripping over him. Quickly, he checked a pulse, and signaled his aide, off stage.

"Now, come help, we will take him with us, it is safer."

Olaf and his aide managed to carry the wounded and groaning speaker off stage before anyone could react. Suffington followed.

A car waited outside, near the door. It was difficult to hoist the wounded man onto the back seat. The aide climbed into the driver's seat, Olaf stayed in back, using hand pressure to control the bleeding. Nigel jumped into the front seat just as it took off, gun pointed.

"Who are you? What do you want?"

"I want to help. I'll tell you where to go. I know a private hospital, no one will find him."

"Did you do this?"

"No. I'm here to protect him."

Olaf's look said good job, that. "And we should trust you now?"

"Don't start, just drive." He kept the gun visible even though he had intention of using it.

# #

Birkstraach hoped the professor was safe but nothing he could do about that now. He had to calm the crowd, now dangerously close to a riot. He quickly moved to the podium, searching for the microphone which had fallen on the floor. Next to it was the Doktor's papers. Automatically, he stuffed them in his jacket pocket, a quick prayer to his recovery. He forgot about the professor, the people had begun shoving each other to get away. He tapped the microphone to get their attention. It had minimal effect but he spoke into it anyway.

"Please, no one leave. There is security already searching for the villain. Please, it is safest in here now. We must wait for the police. Something terrible has happened and we must help them."

A few in the crowd and the photographers managed to rush out before stopped but most paused to listen, curious or unsure, but phones came out and uploads began. He regretted the thought immediately but he had wondered if this would hurt or help their cause.

# #

Joshua moved quickly but Lina's bodyguard had rushed her out the side door; he was not far behind.

In the dim light of the hallway he was maneuvering to retrieve Lina just as she pulled a gun from her purse and shot her bodyguard through the heart. Both men were caught off guard, one went down, eyes wide but empty.

"He deserved that, the pig. Come with me. My limo is waiting. My papa said you would rescue me. Is that right?"

He reached for her gun but she was already running for a rear entrance. The shot would bring onlookers and more danger so he followed her outside where a gray Volvo sedan was parked, motor running, back door open, no other car in sight. At the wheel was a chauffeur in a large cap, face hidden.

"Hold it." He looked around. "Something's wrong. Come with me." He started to pull her away.

"No, you will come with me. I can trust the driver, there is no time."

He started to pull her back but a few reporters had spotted them from the far end of the *Riksdag* and started to run. She was already inside the vehicle.

The door they exited opened, the dead body discovered. He jumped in the car; as he shut the door, the driver sped away. The automatic lock clicked.

That was not his plan. She was up to something but what? A question for later, now they needed distance.

He pulled his gun from the holster, pressed against the neck of the driver.

"To Skavsta airport." The driver didn't react.

Instead, Lina aimed her gun at Joshua. "Give me your gun. You cannot shoot the driver, the car will crash and you will have two murders to explain."

"Two?" He removed the gun from the driver's neck but did not hand it over. She didn't seem to notice.

She smiled. "They will not believe I would do such a thing as to kill my own bodyguard."

"So that's how it is. But why?"

"You always were the clever one but you do not realize that I am clever, too."

Joshua managed a look of mild surprise. "I take it America is out?"

"Oh, I am going to America, just not with you."

"What is it you're planning to do with me? The same as your bodyguard?"

"Not yet, my childhood friend. You have something we want."

"We?"

She nods to the driver. "All in good time. And you will tell us where you have hidden it."

"What is it you think I have that you need so much as to take me for this lovely drive? And at gunpoint? Shotgun wedding?"

"Shotgun? I have a pistol. And I will use it."

He knew she needled easily but this time she went steely. That was a new persona; no longer the spoiled brat of their childhood.

"I don't have anything for you. I was told to bring you to my father's home in America. Your father wanted you safe."

"That horrid man. At least now he is dead. He was going to expose my husband. That would put great stress on his oil rights. Why should my husband be punished by the world stage. What would happen to me?"

"He's your father."

"What father? Where was he when I needed him? No, he went off to make his precious career. You will come, soon, Lina, I promise, you will come soon. Soon, hah, it never came. I was left with that horrible witch of a mother, always drunk, always her men who wanted me."

Whatever kindred feelings he might have had vanished into her malevolent smile, She looked prepared to kill him when she got what she wanted from him. That didn't worry him, he could easily overpower her at some point; the driver, too, since he had to drive but why such an elaborate plan to get back at her father? Why was he even here? It didn't make sense.

"Lina, we need to talk. You're in over your head. I can help you."

"I do not need your help. It is all arranged."

"What? What's arranged?"

"You will know soon. So be quiet. I know you are trying to trick me."

Was it somehow tied into Prague and the computer stick? Why else would she think he had something for her? And what had brought him here? But he couldn't think why she would have anything to do with that assignment. They were separate. Weren't they?

He could easily say it was lost in the river when he fell. Even if they believed him they would just shoot him.

The driver could hear every word and yet showed no interest, continuing to drive but not in the direction of the airport. Whatever she knew about the retrieval of the information on the thumb drive, she'd tell him eventually. She couldn't help bragging. First, though, he wanted to know who was behind the planning that almost got him and his partner killed. He began to suspect it involved a lot more than a few computer files. He'd been briefed on the assignment but as far as he knew, neither of them knew the contents.

If this was about Prague and she knew who had set them up then why bring him to Stockholm? Getting to his father would be easy enough, for no one else did Bennett Daine jump like he did for Yurovinsky. It was more than just friendship, his father was too pragmatic for that.

Two supposedly unrelated events. The computer stick? He knew Valerie would have taken his warning seriously and hidden it. He couldn't think what else Lina, or anyone, could want from him now. He and Valerie had been on separate assignments for the month prior, basic intel gathering, nothing that would interest anyone until the bits were put together by analysts. Need to know, compartmentalize, company policy. Nothing unusual in that, unless he was about to uncover information someone wanted kept secret. On the retrieved package? Was that it? Something else?

What was on it that would bring Lina to harm her father? Or him, for that matter, although he certainly had his detractors. Was she even involved or, more likely, just the messenger? She was greedy and clever about getting what she wanted but long term planning was not her interest, instant gratification suited her. So who had instant access to their changed location and why did it involve Lina and her father?

Suddenly, he was very worried about Valerie. He'd left a message on the burner phone that would bring her over if she didn't hear from him soon. Iif he had uncovered something she would be put in unknown danger. Or maybe he was the bait and she was the target. Maybe Lina wasn't asking about the computer stick but about his partner. Her English could easily mix up something for someone.

Joshua's brain began to swirl. Lina's mouth moved but he could near nothing.

# #

Chapter 12

The midday weather in New York City was perfect. No wind to muss the wedding party's hair, no heat that would make morning coats unbearable. St. Francis Xavier church in Midtown Manhattan with its stunning Baroque exterior surpassed only by the frescoes and golden lighting of the interior. Weddings were popular not just for the service but for the photos.

The milling and late arriving guests were finally seated, ushers took their place at the altar, the two flower girls were given final instructions and from the waiting limo the bride stepped out. A vision in Vera Wang white, she was beaming in her joy. Bennett almost lapsed into yearning for his wife not living long enough to give him a daughter until he caught himself, not the day for regrets.

The music began. A few passersby on the sidewalk stopped to watch. Over the church organ playing the traditional wedding march Bennett escorted the bride down the aisle behind two flower girls, solemn in their importance. Behind them were six bridesmaids, resplendent in peach-tulle belted A-line knee length gowns topped by a haku lei of plumeria and white roses for their hair.

Cortina d'Angelo, in a one-off Caroline Herrera pale orange flared silk spring dress with embroidered flowers, and hat to match, watched them from the front, tears in her eyes. Geoffrey Palmer, the groom, in his first tux bought for him by his grandmother whose husband had been a tailor, waited, confident he had scored the winning lottery ticket. Not only was his almost wife smart and funny and ridiculously beautiful but she was rich. He knew his father cheated on his mother and he made a vow right then he would never cheat on Deirdre. His mood bordered on giddy and he fought to control himself. Time enough for that later.

He had briefly met the man walking her down the aisle at the family dinner, Deidre had said she barely knew him, some friend of her mother's; he was okay, her father had known him. Geoff thought he seemed preoccupied but he knew of his reputation, no doubt thinking of another zillion dollar deal about to close. Geoff smiled, life was seriously good.

As the wedding party arrived at the altar the priest raised his hand for the benediction. At the back of the huge cathedral Bernmeister stepped out, to take a phone call. No one noticed.

#   #

Valerie paid the taxi driver and hurried up the steps to Bernmeister, pacing, wearing a dark suit and mirrored sunglasses. She had changed and cleaned up, wearing pants, shirt and casual jacket, dark glasses, ball cap with a backpack. She looked like a nearby New School student, always in a rush. Not much of a disguise but the DC-NY train is full of people too preoccupied to notice anyone who couldn't help their careers.

"Took you long enough."

"A little matter of blood stained clothes so you'll get a bill from a Target store, lucky one of your guys knew the night guard. Very handy when your boss' brain matter ruins that perfect outfit. Why here?"

"Wedding thing."

"Bennett Daine is getting married?"

"No." He pointed. "Stand over there."

Deciding a retort would be wasted she moved aside as the bride and groom rushed out, laughing. Right behind came the wedding party, feeling released after the long ceremony. The guests then filed out and after various selfies, and of course the traditional bouquet toss grabbed by a woman who clearly had her eyes on one of the groomsmen, left in a dozen or so limos for the four block ride to the reception. The mayor brought his own security vehicle. A few celebrities mingled with other celebrities. Valerie watched it all, knowing that might have been her in another lifetime.

The wedding party held back for official photos. Bennett had seen Rod and behind him, Valerie. His eyes briefly flashed concern but he kept his smile for the camera and for Corie, who was beaming.

Once everyone had left Rod said, without turning to Valerie."We'll walk." She might not like him but she had no doubt he knew what he was doing. She hoisted her backpack and followed.

At the hotel he stuck her in the kitchen but at least they fed her while she waited, some mishaps of prep deemed unsuitable for actual guests. How do people work in a place with such madness? In and out with trays, banging pots, a chef yelling his creations were being ruined by amateurs and at least four languages she could hear. Oddly, all seemed remarkably happy with their employment situation. Go figure.

An hour or so later Bernmeister returned for her. A bare nod of his head which seemed to be his version of follow me. He made Joshua seem a babbling brook of chatter. They stood in the back of the large reception room as Bennett gave a toast, to intermittent applause. Finally, he raised his glass, said something she couldn't quite hear, some laughter followed and then said for all to hear:

"Salud. Geoffrey and Deirdre, may your lives always be filled with the same joy that's in your eyes today." The bride and groom stood, to applause, and thanked everyone for coming. Geoff took her hand and they walked around the dais to the dance floor.

Already set up at the side of the room was an orchestra that began singing a version of "You and Me" like the Dave Mathews Band. Valerie looked closer, it was the Dave Mathews Band. She tapped Bernmeister's shoulder and pointed. With zero interest he said, "friends of the groom." It had been years since she'd danced with a man, or been invited to a party, suddenly sad for the life she had been forced to leave behind. But she didn't think the man next to her was into nostalgia. Or dancing.

After giving the couple their moment, Bennett held out his hand to Corie. She smiled and followed him and they began to dance, soon followed by other couples. Daine, aware of the urgency, whispered in Corie's ear. She smiled gamely and permitted him to lead her towards the ballroom exit. Rod pulled Valerie outside while his boss gave his apology, kissed Corie on the cheek and allowed a moment to excuse himself. She nodded and wished him well.

Daine joined them in the hall and they walked quickly to a waiting car outside.

Inside the moving car, Bennett looked to Rod. "Where is my son?"

"He's with Lina. There were shots. Yevi was hit but he's on his way to a private clinic, under the radar. If he's still alive he'll get good care, I was assured of that."

Daine allowed himself a moment to process that. "And?"

Bernmeister looked at Valerie. "My boss was shot. She was taking me somewhere, at gunpoint, in the company parking garage. Someone blew her… she's down. I left in a hurry, no time to explain."

Daine spoke. "You're being hunted?"

"Yes."

To Rod. "Alternate landing secured?"

"Yessir."

"Nigel have a safe house?"

"Yessir."

"Wait, I'm not going to a…."

They both looked at her. Daine spoke, not politely. "It's not a leap to presume you'll head for your partner. I don't want you anywhere near him right now." He softened his voice. "It's safer for both of you. And we'll know where you are, if needed. Better that than too many after the same target."

He made sense, she had to give him that.

"Give me all the details. Plenty of time, it's a long flight."

Two hours later, on the Daine Gulfstream G650, Valerie was dead to the world. The leather seating was more comfortable than her bed, roomier, too. The smooth ride would have lulled her even if she hadn't had a long day and no sleep. She'd told what she could, Rod could fill in the rest.

"Then Lina went with him willingly?"

"She was seen leaving with her bodyguard as soon as the shots were fired, Joshua right behind."

"Then he's safe?"

"As far as we know. They drove off in a gray sedan, her driver." He didn't mention the bodyguard was found in the hallway, dead. That information came from another ex-military hire, posing as a reporter.

"Any idea who shot Yevi?"

"What I've been able to piece together so far, the shots, two, came as the professor was about to expose names involved in some kind of an environmental cover up. It may be unrelated but it's a starting point. Nigel saw him carried offstage and followed. His orders are to stay with him until he hears from me. If he can get that list of names I can run down any possibilities."

"I'm concerned Joshua hasn't called. Check your phone again."

Daine was so used to 24/7 communication he forgot their phone embargo on the plane, the wifi risk slight but enough. Rod, too, was desperate for updates. But any breach and locations might be compromised. Still, Bernmeister checked.

"He'll wait until he's clear and has something to report. Security would be his primary concern now."

"Yes, of course. You're right." Bernmeister was surprised that his boss was so frightened for his son, he knew Joshua's ability. He had no idea what issues the two men had but he could guess. Not his problem, though, his job was to keep everyone focused, especially his boss.

"He's with Lina. He'll protect her."

Bernmeister, after talking to Joshua the other night when he stopped by, had done a deep dive into Lina and her relationship to her father but he did not share his findings, that Lina was not to be trusted at all.

Joshua was on his own. That didn't worry him much; of more concern was why.

# #

The physical therapist who had gotten Nigel on his feet with a combination of understanding and brute force was eventually undone with all the war wounded that crossed his path. An asthmatic, Terrace Rubenstein still remembered the day he realized his mother had misspelled his name on the birth certificate. He didn't much like Terry or Rube so he settled on Buck, from Buck Rogers, a movie he'd happened to see the day he wanted a new name. Eventually it stuck. He didn't much like Rubenstein either so one day he walked into the Registrar's office and changed it legally to Buck Rogers. Most people assumed it was a nickname and he never corrected them.

Working in physical therapy in a veteran's facility put him near a lot of drugs and it didn't take long for him to test the samples always being dropped off. Highs and lows, he soon became an expert. Too much of one. He was fired and lost his license and reputation. Eventually

177

he wound up in a tiny clinic outside Stockholm that mostly did abortions and plastic surgery at discounted rates and mostly off the books. When it was closed down a newly minted doctor fresh out of medical school, wanting to make a difference not buckets of money, took over. Soon it became a well respected neighborhood clinic.

Buck was allowed to stay on, he had valuable skills, as long as he stayed off drugs. With a new home and respect, he had. He and Nigel had kept in touch, two outcasts that understood the crawl out of oblivion.

So when Nigel had called about a gunshot victim kept on the down low as his life was in danger, he spoke to Doctor Fassbinder who agreed, reluctantly, to not file the report immediately. It was after hours anyway, he could manage a day or so, behind in paperwork. And the extra money would certainly help the clinic.

Olaf and his aide helped get Yurovinsky on the table. Dr. Fassbinder did a quick evaluation. He'd lost a lot of blood and he was not in the best shape but he could remove the bullet and, if no further internal damage, put him on penicillin. After that, he would monitor but it was up to the patient. He shooed everyone out.

Olaf called Birkstraach. Doktor Yurovinsky was being treated, but needed privacy. He would be in touch when he knew more. No, he couldn't say more at this time. Nigel had mentioned the doktor's papers but Birkstraach couldn't remember, said he had no idea but would look.

Nigel left them to it and went outside to call Rod. It went to voicemail. He didn't leave a message.

# #

Rather than fight against another episode Joshua decided to relax, hoping it would lessen the impact. The timing might be lousy but he could probably pass it off as disinterest. He let his mind drift back.

Right off the bat Valerie had annoyed him. Their assignment was an art theft in a small Parisian gallery in the sixth *arrondissement* where, it turned out, she had lived for a while after training. She knew the language and the shortcuts through *ruelles* or back alleys. While the area had gentrified over the years a few of the old shopkeepers remembered her while disdaining him, an Englishman in their eyes. She belonged, he didn't.

The art theft wasn't their concern, the *Sureté* had a team assigned but the gallery was considered a conduit in a money laundering scheme running through several Eastern European banks not regulated by U.S. laws. French and Italian galleries and shops had become the final wash on the path to U.S. banks. Their job was to discover and plug the spigot.

Adding to his irritation her old roommate, Juliette something, was living with an artist and three or four hundred kids based on the noise through the wall. L'Etienne, a pretentious name even for an artist, knew the owner of the suspect gallery, had in fact displayed his paintings and gotten a good price for them. Joshua was cranky enough by then to tell him it had been due to money laundering inflation but Valerie, more sensitive to the assignment, and feelings, had admired his work, even bought one of their old neighborhood. By the end of the day, during a hearty meal of cassoulet and bottles of wine they'd brought, she had all the information necessary for the legal team to shut them down. Worse, enough of the players cut a deal that four more illicit financial pathways were also cut off.

Naturally, the brass were thrilled with their partnership. Assignments became more complex. He regained footing as she recognized his experience had value and he accepted that her insight provided clarity.

Gradually his fear for her safety became manageable. She knew her job, she would find a way here without attracting attention. That's what she did and did well. He could protect her best by learning who had found a way into Lina's greedy little heart enough that she would kill.

"What are you doing?" She kicked his feet. Being ignored was not her favorite thing.

"You said to be quiet. If you'd like to speak, please do."

"I don't want to speak. You need to tell me where is your little computer thing."

"Computer thing?" One question answered.

"The one you stole. Or that shabby little girl you work with did but she was supposed to give it to you. So you should have it because she was searched."

"Oh, that." He stretched his legs, away from her. Call her shabby one more time and I'll pull your hair out with pliers. Aloud, he said, "I turned it over when I returned. You can ask them. I can't promise they're tell you, though."

"Now you are just being stupid. If they had it they would not have asked me to get it." He stared at her. She actually thought she mattered to them. Not that he cared too much but he was certain if he handed it over she'd be dead seconds after she gave it to them. But who was "*them?*" He had to get her to share that much. Saving her life was further down the list.

The driver, seemingly oblivious to their conversation, followed impossible to pronounce streets through the afternoon traffic, turning often, not rushing but clearly with a destination in mind.

Eventually they crossed *Söldertäljevägen* bridge and passed a sign that said Lake *Mälaren*, one of the larger water bodies that ended in the Baltic Sea. He remembered that from his map reading. It was on the southwestern side of the Stockholm archipelago in an area called *Hägersten-Liljeholmen*. *Mälar*, as it was sometimes called, runs along the northern border; it's eastern end connects with *Södermalm*, a more expensive suburb, just south of city centre. Sports were part of the culture there with five arenas to play in, adding to the soccer, or fotboll, rosters of Europe.

Sweden consisted of thousands of islands, not all inhabited; some urban, some forest. From space satellites it must have looked like a blue carpet onto which had spilled green and white confetti of differing sizes. While most Stockholm districts had their own character, to an outsider it all looked alike: water around land stuffed with high rise apartments and connected by bridges. He missed Valerie, she had the internal directional signal of a homing pigeon. When he was with her they never got lost, another of her annoying habits. At least he was a strong swimmer and as spring was here he probably wouldn't freeze to death if he could find a way to jump in the lake.

No time for fanciful thoughts, he had to stay sharp. The driver now had his attention, something was familiar about him though from behind he couldn't see his face under the cap.

Lina was nattering on about something.

"... and they will find you, alas, dead, with the gun that killed my poor unsuspecting guard in your hand."

"I thought you wanted a computer thing that you think I have although you know more than I do about that." Did she really think she had the upper hand?

The bad news was that no one knew where he was. He and Lina were supposed to be on a plane heading for home. His father would be with Yevi although he hadn't seen him at the speech. They'd agreed no contact but now it was a concern.

His father would likely have been backstage, to greet Yevi when he finished, get him safely away. But someone had killed the lights and shots were fired; Lina said her father was dead. Was he the intended target and were the shots to stop the speech or the speaker? Or something else entirely and where did his father fit in? Lina was involved in something beyond her understanding but was her father also somehow involved? Supposedly it was two unrelated events but was it? And if connected, how?

He had to get a message to Bernmeister. He'd asked him to get some information on Lina, her connections and more specifically, her husband, a Russian oligarch, crooked by definition. Valerie would wait for an all clear from him and when he didn't return she'd find a way over. He wasn't sure that was a good idea under the circumstances but he also didn't know how to stop her.

He'd been in worse situations, too many times. That didn't concern him so much but he started to wonder if he might just be the bait for something else.

Right now he had too many questions and too few answers. Like it or not Lina was the only one who could help.

He shifted slightly, to better remove her gun if it came to that. In doing so the driver noticed and he caught a glimpse in the rear view mirror. This time he recognized the bridge of the nose, a slight indent from a long ago bullet, a wound that could have easily been fixed with plastic surgery but was kept to awe people when they learned he had faced - literally - a bullet and won.

That changed everything; he now knew who was behind this, someone he knew was capable of the most diabolical planning, a legend nearly equal to his own. Past his prime, yes, but dangerous all the same.

Aaron Beckman was man who had at his disposal all the world's secrets. He knew exactly what was on the computer file and he either wanted to destroy the information or blackmail someone.

And that meant his father would be the bait to get him to give it up. That's why his father was invited to Stockholm and the story of Lina's defection created.

Lina was staring out of the window, bored. Her gun dangled from her fingers but he couldn't just grab it and blast his way out without knowing his father was safe.

He was sure the driver of the car knew his whereabouts. He would have to wait.

As if reading his mind, he finally spoke. "So Agent Daine. You have figured this out. I thought you might."

Early evening but the sun still bright as the gray Volvo sedan pulled up to a small house tucked away behind a larger house. It was painted a bright yellow with green trim but with scaffolding along one side, not yet completed. It was a small but lovely house, in a area undergoing renovation. The workday was finishing, workers were leaving, not paying much attention to an arriving car. Beckman pulled the car into the tiny detached garage.

"Take his gun. I doubt he's going to shoot you with so many witnesses."

"Shoot kidnappers? Not a problem."

"Shoot your father's godchild? For all your toughness you have that wasted heart of gold. Too much money, that's your problem. Never had to scramble to eat."

Joshua knew about Beckman, too. He was N.S.A. when he was in training, a devoted war hawk, not liked but effective. A weak president had hired him as his National Security Adviser, to be the *cojoñes* he lacked. He'd been fired and hired a number of times since then. He'd overstepped boundaries, endured Congressional investigations but had always slipped through to disappear for a while, trying to gin up converts wherever he could. Then another president, too indecisive to go to war, would hire him, sending him out as the chum into his administration's empty water.

Beckman's claim to fame if you could call it that was his humongous Bowie knife strapped to his waist. He never flew commercial and so was never without it. He'd become quite proficient with it, loved to flip it at a wall next to some unsuspecting underling who'd said something he'd deemed unworthy. His staff feared him as much as the knife. He cut no slack. Only when a woman he wanted to bed appeared did he turn on the charm. Most were ambitious, he could place them in positions from which to rise. Turn him down and you were never seen in his department again. Years of career momentum lost. Even in progressive days of women's workplace power, none would speak up and risk, well, he was dangerous. Rumors began to swirl of women never heard from again when they'd likely tired of the machismo of Washington and returned home to more civilized jobs.

True to form, he'd used the rumors to advance his reputation as someone you don't mess with. He'd lie just for practise or to protect his position, it made no difference to him. Few knew of his upbringing but few doubted he was the problem child.

Truth be told he was hardly the poor boy he made out to be although not rich. He was a bad seed, some said, and his parents had sent him to a distant cousin's military academy where he proceeded to bully the younger cadets. Their training kept them quiet, as such his reputation for evil grew. Beckman loved it. If the devil were looking for an assistant, he'd found one in Aaron Beckman.

Joshua was less enamored of the man's reputation. He was just a greedy son of a bitch with no real talent.

As with most bullies they used force without subtlety and could spot a victim across a crowded room. He knew who would be swayed by fear before they even spoke. He knew exactly where to go to get the best deal for himself. It was sometimes called narcissism although Joshua thought asshole pretty well covered it.

Inside the house, a few mismatched chairs and ratty sofa by a dirty fireplace was the only furniture. A coffee pot sat on a counter in the kitchen area through the far door. Lina had a gun on him and he could take it from her in one move but Beckman had a play and he was curious. He wasn't afraid of Beckman either but he also knew the man would kill for no reason. He'd seen the knife in action and was pretty sure he couldn't outrun it.

Beckman said, "This is your father's house, did you know that?"

Both turned to him, unsure which father he meant. "That's right." He nodded to Lina. "Your father bought it for his father. A present." He nodded at Joshua. "One big happy family." He laughed. A back tooth was missing and not replaced.

Lina's eyes lit up. "He's dead so it belongs to me. I won't give it to anyone. It's mine. You see, Joshua, you can't have what belongs to me."

"Then I guess it's your house. I hope you two have many happy years here."

Lina isn't sure if he means it. Beckman even manages a smile, not of mirth.

"Now, what's for dinner? Sorry, Daine, but you'll be tied up. You can't be trusted with a sandwich in your hands."

"If we're going out, I must freshen up."

He went cold. "Go make sandwiches. I left a bag in the kitchen. And hurry up about it."

She stared at him, ready to argue, decided not.

#   #

Chapter 13

As the sun rose over the Baltic Sea it streamed into the plane's interior, waking the dozing passengers. Daine had retreated to the private room in back with an actual bed although he'd barely slept. This assignment, something his son had done many times, then Yevi's shooting, not knowing what had happened and why, but his priority was to get Lina out of the country. He would stick to that, unless the situation changed. His nerves were raw, having connected with his son, the thought of losing him was intolerable.

As the plane began it's descent he decided to pass his worries off as age, a father ready to make amends. Easier said than done but it was better for all if he behaved normally and compartmentalized his thoughts.

In the main cabin Bernmeister stood and stretched. He nudged Valerie who, trained in outside interference, was instantly alert. The cabin attendant brought strong coffee followed by a platter of meats and cheese and rolls.

After landing and a cursory customs check, a vetted driver was waiting in a hired car and drove to the safe house Nigel had chosen, a three bedroom apartment in *Södermalm*, on the second floor in one of the brightly painted pale yellow buildings overlooking the water, a common view on an island. Online research had suggested the trendy suburb would be crowded with tourists as spring brought long days after a dark winter and fragrant lilac bushes burst onto the scene. It offered easy access to the city centre and a hide in plain sight venue, safe was the operative word.

Nigel, in preparation for their arrival, had left some tee shirts and athletic wear with logos of Hammarby IF, the local fotboll team, using that as an excuse to catch a game. Hammarby *Sjöstad* was just the other side and across the bay and *Södermalm* residents loved their home team; they would blend easily. He was rather proud of himself for that little touch and hoped it was all right but Rod's text they'd arrived was terse so he'd only responded in kind with his location and the professor's dire but hopeful outlook.

Daine, however, was still too concerned about his friend's condition to notice. He knew Bernmeister was doing what he could but he also knew he needed to get his own handle on things. He went straight to the larger bedroom with en suite. He shut the door and called a number he rarely used, for emergencies only. This qualified.

He left a brief cryptic message. Within the hour Monroe Kellenstone III, Deputy Director of the C.I.A. through four administrations, most recently tumultuous leading to speculation he was on his way out, returned his call. They went back years more as business associates with occasional use for each other rather than friends.

"Bennett. You've landed. Good."

"Even for you, that's quick."

"I have access to FAA reports, or did you forget?"

"Then you know what happened here. Do you know by whom? I was supposed to be here yesterday for the speech."

"I have a pretty good idea but still getting the intel. Do you know where he is?"

"Yes."

"Any news?"

Not that he'd share with the C.I.A., friend or not. "No, not yet."

Monroe paused, he knew better. "Bennett, you need me on this one. I have a lot to tell you. Can we meet?"

"Tell me one thing. Are you behind any of this?"

"I can be there for dinner."

Monroe Kellenstone hung up the phone. Years in Washington after field work mostly in Eastern Europe, he was well versed in the world's secrets, who could be trusted and who could not. He rarely thought about his youth, fresh out of law school who had wanted to save the world. Both his parents had been teachers and he loved them and it was a loving household but to his mind, boring. He wanted so much more to his life. His father had never understood his wild streak, not getting into trouble so much as testing his limits. His mother, he felt, had understood but would never break ranks with her husband. He had two older sisters who alternately ignored him, resented babysitting him and practised makeup tricks on him. He was too young to see anything wrong with it and liked the attention. Perhaps it's where the seeds of change to suit the purpose at hand began to sprout.

Sports weren't really his thing but history was and he loved his toy soldiers almost as much as his family. He'd named them, sacrificed a few in his battles and spent many happy hours that, in his mind, made the world a safer place. His sisters eventually moved on, first to college then to marriage. He was an uncle, he couldn't remember how many times over but thankfully Midget, his diminutive secretary, had it all down in her book, kept so secret even the C.I.A. head didn't know what was in it. He'd often suspected that one day she'd publish it for all to see. Or use it for blackmail. He'd teased her about that once and she'd been furious. He had never done it again. Humor did not reside in her.

She was actually named Margaret but he'd never thought of her as anything but Midget. At first she'd thought it demeaning but after nearly twenty years together they had each other's back. She never revealed classified information or any information for that matter to anyone but him. He, off the books, had seen that her alcoholic husband moved to the other coast leaving her the house, two kids and a quiet divorce, never to be heard from again. Monroe knew a few tricks and like most bullies, the man frightened easily. Her two kids moved to the uncle pile so they had a male role model. Midget never married again, he never married at all and while there had been moments over the years when something might have happened between them, one or the other saw that it didn't. Maybe because of the one secret no one but Midget knew, his only other off the books activity.

Until last year, when one of his long ago contacts from the Soviet Union had resurfaced and let him know someone had been snooping. He'd been out of the office on his annual holiday from the Archives and knew his replacement so hadn't bothered to check thoroughly on his return. Only by accident, looking for something had he come across the request form. It could be nothing of course but in their line of work, Dimitri had been an informant in the old days, nothing was often something. Monroe had always protected him and here he was on the verge of a pension. Not a happy life really but better than most of his family and friends. In Russia, happiness was too often found in a bottle of vodka. He and his wife did not drink. They read books and babysat their grandchildren.

Monroe could decide if the information mattered to him. They communicated infrequently but he knew how to contact him, an online flower shop with encrypted instructions for pickup. Conveniently, his anniversary was soon, his wife would be pleased even though she'd fuss that he spent too much.

It turned out that the information given to Monroe mattered, a lot.

He grabbed his always ready travel case, pondering as he left how much to tell Daine about his son.

# #

Valerie was debating how much information to share with Bernmeister. She knew his loyalty was to the Daine family, specifically Joshua's father. She also knew he would protect Joshua as part of that loyalty. But he was her partner, it was her job to find and protect him.

The safe house was comfortable. Now she wondered why they were there. The last word they'd had on Joshua was that he and Lina had gotten away. His father believed both were safely on their way to America and was concerned only with that professor friend of his. She looked at Rod, pretty sure he shared her concerns. It was not a clean getaway and there were shots fired. Joshua would never use gunfire as diversion in a roomful of people. That meant someone else had alternate ideas.

Because of the message on the prepaid phone he was making her aware of his situation. If he didn't contact her she would know where to go. While his communication skills could be sparse he never ignored a follow up when he'd left coded instructions. He knew she'd drop everything to find him and he hadn't told her to stay put.

A tourist guidebook gave her confirmation. Clearly, Uncle Bernie was Berns Hotel, in the center of Stockholm. That's where she needed to be. If he was okay and couldn't use a phone he would have left a message of some sort. If not, something was wrong.

Bernmeister was standing in the doorway, watching her.

"He left a message when he first arrived." She held up the phone. "If he didn't report back it would be at the Berns Hotel. I checked. It's not far from here."

"I've already ordered backup to cover Mr. Daine. I'll take you."

She debated only a few seconds but decided this wasn't the time to be territorial. She nodded.

The location, at *Näckströmsgatan* 8 between *Kungsträdgården* and *Berzelii* Parks was just across *Strömbron* bridge, was about a twenty minute drive.

194

Parking, however, was another matter but Rod seemed unconcerned and stopped to have the valet keep the car close, a man to man thing, probably thinking he was married and they were having a noon quickie.

Inside the ornate lobby with its splashes of red and a long narrow bar that had the most ornate chandeliers this side of Versailles seemed incongruous for a place that valued discretion. She decided the direct approach would work best.

"Valerie Rhodes, do you have a message for me, please?"

The clerk glanced discreetly at Bernmeister, standing off to the side checking out anyone who might show too much interest. After a few moments at the computer, he said, "Yes. Mr. Daine checked out but left this." He retreated to a side area and returned with an envelope he handed over.

"Thank you."

Outside, she read the contents aloud. "We'll always have Paris." She looked at Rod. "That's not good."

"Meaning?"

"Meaning he expected something to go wrong. If he were on the plane he would send an okay. This is our code for stand by."

"Maybe that's all it is, to wait."

Valerie looked at him as if to say she wasn't that stupid, so don't insult her.

He said, "I checked the airport, no flight manifest matching his went out. He's still in the country, unless they left by boat."

They looked around; from almost any vantage point on this island capital water was visible. In fact, Rod thought, if he were leaving Sweden on the down low he'd do it by boat. Air travel brought attention, by sea not so much. One could appear to be going for a sail and meet up with a larger yacht or, with a few discreet contacts, cross into Denmark without anyone knowing.

He left her to her thoughts and walked off to make some calls. Bernmeister had, over the years, accumulated almost as many contacts as his boss. Not the same caliber but in his opinion if you wanted real information you went lower down the food chain. Documents were never eyes only, someone had to type, to copy, to fax, to messenger and all had the potential to be known by other than eyes only. Those were not traitors, not for money but for a trusted colleague who had done them favors. Rod made sure he did a lot of favors.

His childhood in west Texas had been tough. More than tough, his father, a farmer who'd barely scraped by, drank away whatever small pittance he'd managed to earn, worked his kids nearly to death, foregoing school, and often beating them. Rod, as the oldest, did his best to cover for the younger ones, a boy and a girl. His mother had eventually given up, she couldn't stop him. In those days there was no place for an abused wife to go, courts had few laws, even if proof could be had.

One day in the fields his father, in a particularly nasty mood, went off to shoot a squirrel for dinner. Rod heard a shot and then a shout. He'd hesitated, not wanting to face the wrath of his father if he'd missed; having used his rifle as a club more than once and once it had gone off, missing him by inches.

When Bernmeister arrived his father was writhing on the ground, having tripped on an exposed tree root, his leg bleeding. He knew how to apply a tourniquet but instead had sat on a nearby log, maybe forty minutes, watching his father die a slow agonizing death, screaming at him to get help. Rod knew if his father survived there would be hell to pay but he didn't care. Like his mother he'd reached the end.

Eventually his father passed. Rod walked back to the house and called the Sheriff who came out. He was no fool and had more than a suspicion what had happened. Footprints for one thing. Rod saw him checking them out where his feet had shuffled by the log and braced himself for what was to come. Instead, the Sheriff heard the ambulance arrive from the next county, supervised the removal of the body and left. Rod returned home and told the rest of the family what had happened. No one said a thing but ate the potato soup, with an egg from one of the chickens, all they had without the squirrel.

The next day neighbors brought food, real food, casseroles and pies and even a ham. The youngest had never tasted ham and ate so much she threw up. Never had the family been so happy. Even his mother managed a smile.

Neighbors continued to bring food and clothes and talked of putting the kids in school. It was the law but rarely enforced in farm country. For a while Rod had tried to keep the farm going but without proper irrigation or seeds it was impossible. When the Sheriff returned, he spent a lot of time with his mother. She'd been increasingly ill, years of deprivation taking a toll. There was a home for wayward mothers, what they still called pregnant teenagers in west Texas. She could help out part time for room and board. But not her children.

The Sheriff's sister had a friend, childless, who wanted the younger two. She felt they were still salvageable. Rod, devastated, had encouraged them to go, a huge opportunity. He was 17 now, he'd manage on his own. But the Sheriff had pulled him aside, the army had a program, he could enlist and get an education, a high school equivalency and a career. He knew it was the best offer he would get. And he never forgot that man's kindness to his family.

Valerie suddenly stood and headed back into the hotel. Her purposeful walk reminded him of his young sister, she had that same stride. In some ways he thought it might be why he did what he did; knowing their father would certainly destroy her curiosity with his constant belittling and lack of education would lessen her chances. He missed his siblings but after a few visits the adoptive family made it clear they'd prefer he stayed away. They were now a nuclear family and he was their past. By then he was away most of the time and they had few memories of their early days. He had kept tabs on them, sent money at Christmas, but otherwise let them be.

He caught up to her. "What?"

"We can't stay here forever but he needs to know we've been here. You and I are renting a room. Let them think I cheat on him. They won't tell."

Inside she let him play his part. He rented a room, on a lower floor, "for a couple of nights," they'd hang out the do not disturb sign. And find a way to let Joshua know where she was.

She knew exactly what that would be.

Two hours later she was done. If he was unencumbered he would find her. If not, well, frankly that was his job. Whatever problems he'd encountered he damn well better find a way out and soon. She was tired of always rescuing him. He took too many chances just to show off. It was always his fault, it was.....

"Are you all right? You look a little..."

"What?" She said, louder than necessary.

Slightly surprised, he shrugged. Now she reminded him of his wife. What was with his trip down memory lane? He had to shut that down, now.

"Good. Let's go."

Asking where seemed a bad idea so he followed, having watched her prepare the room. She had sent him to a nearby department store for three large towels, bath sheets she called them, in a medium shade of blue, white and red, no patterns or stripes, and clothespins or some kind of fasteners, large binder clips would do. The only red towel had a pattern but the backside was plain, he hoped that would do. He was not used to taking orders from a woman and found, no surprise, he didn't much like it.

She grabbed the towels and dumped all three in the tub without removing the tags then turned on the tap. When they were soaked through she carried them, dripping, to the balcony and hung them over the railing to dry and secured with the fasteners. He stared a minute and then he got it, right to left - blue, white, red - opposite order from outside. For the first time since she'd appeared from the rock formation he was impressed. Paris on the note meant to wait and the colors of the French flag were a reference to that and in which room. Those two really were joined at the hip. He wasn't ready to admit it but he was jealous of such a close relationship.

On the desk she drew a fire on the notepad by the phone. She pressed hard on the pen, even added a marshmallow on a stick to match the stick person holding it. She ripped it off, tore into pieces, stuck in her pocket but left the pad, and the indentations. That, no matter how much he tried to decipher, didn't click.

"Out."

He thought she meant just him but she followed, putting the Do Not Disturb sign on the door.

At the car she let him pay the valet but she got in the driver's seat. "You drive too slow. Get in."

Wanting to contribute as she risked life and limb zooming through traffic he said, "I had someone check CCTV cameras and they picked up a gray sedan leaving the scene but no driver visible."

"Well?"

"Well, what?"

"Your friend, the one who has the professor. I want to know what he knows."

"I want to get back to Mr. Daine."

"Right now I want to see that professor. His daughter left with my partner, and he hasn't checked in."

Rod didn't respond. A lot of reasons for that, none he wanted to share while she was driving like a maniac. But he picked up the phone and called Nigel, who was relieved to hear from him and more relieved to know he was nearby.

At the clinic, about halfway to Malmö in southern Sweden, was probably more than the hour or so it took her as she pulled into the single remaining parking stall of the tiny stand alone building. Rod, amazed they weren't stopped even with lax European speed limits, followed her to meet Nigel, in reception. He led the way to Professor Yurovinsky's small but spotless room, where they found him, unconscious, with a saline drip in his arm and oxygen tube under his nose.

Dr. Fassbinder finished checking his patient to talk to them. "Are you family?"

"No. His daughter is with my partner and they are missing. I'm hoping he can tell us where they would go."

"I doubt it. He's not very responsive. I've sedated him, the bullet hit a small vein, he lost a lot of blood. He was brought here just in time." He glanced at Nigel, not thrilled at his predicament. "I haven't reported the bullet wound yet but I can't stall much longer without an investigation. I won't risk my clinic."

Rod spoke. "I can take care of that. My boss will make a call if necessary. Through the weekend, that's all we need."

Valerie started to object but he silenced her with his hand. "I will see that he's moved before Monday to a hospital, you can say he was too weak to move and your paperwork was in order."

The doctor nodded, still not happy but Bernmeister handed him an envelope that had what appeared to be a great deal of money, medicine for his patients that could not afford treatment.

Valerie raised her eyebrows at that gesture or that he was so prepared. Rod shrugged, his line of work.

Dr. Fassbinder said, "I have other patients to see. Please, remember he is ill. I cannot promise he will survive until Monday. The antibiotics are not working as well as I'd hoped. He was not a man in good health."

"Thank you, Doctor." Buck appeared in the doorway, Nigel joined him off to the side to chat. Olaf sat by the window, his aide having left. He looked barely awake but had no intention of leaving.

Valerie ignored them, stared at Yurovinsky. She thought a minute then leaned down and said, "Father? Father, can you hear me?"

The old man stirred. "My Lina? Is that you?" His voice was weak, barely a whisper.

"Yes, Father. I need help."

"Your Uncle Bennett, he will help you."

"I cannot find him. He is with his son. Do you know where they are? I will go to them."

Yurovinsky seemed to drift out of what little consciousness he was able to muster. Olaf looked like he wanted to intervene but one look from Bernmeister and he sat back down.

"A house. When Bennett was a boy, he lived in a house, before they moved to England. I bought it last year, as a surprise for him. I have to tell him, I have to tell him what happened. I kept his secret but he has to know. He has to know. Will you bring him to me?"

"Yes, Father, I will do that. Tell me where is this house?"

But Yurovinsky had used his last breath. She checked, he still had a pulse but it was weak. Buck entered. "You have to go now. He'll sleep, maybe wake again, but not soon."

Outside, Rod told Nigel to stay with him, let him know if any change. They returned to the car where Rod insisted on driving since they were returning to the safe house. He had to check on Mr. Daine.

She didn't object. Her only thought was how to find Joshua and if Bennett Daine remembered the location of his early home.

# #

Monroe Kellenstone showed his credentials at the door of the address Bennett Daine had given him. As safe houses went it was a good choice. Private entrance, middle floor, active neighborhood, easy to dissolve into crowds, if needed. The guard recognized Kellenstone on sight but checked the credentials thoroughly, wanting to seem professional.

"Go right in, sir, he's expecting you."

"Thank you."

Kellenstone had known Daine for nigh on forty years. Daine, using his investment firm as a cover, had done intermittent work for the company over the years. He had many contacts and was trusted. He'd grown up in England although Kellenstone was aware he was a foreign adoption. Few knew that but he did a deep dive before trusting him. He'd told no one and never discussed it with Daine. None of his business and his new parents were legitimate. He respected the man a great deal but their lives diverged and had little in common.

Today, though, he would have to trust him more than he ever had. He would trust him with his own past.

It was that past that brought them to this point and his guilt was threatening to derail everything. That's why he had to trust Daine. Someone had to do the thinking; his mind was clouded.

The wrinkle in that was Daine's son was missing. That would cloud Daine's thinking. Old men, too many memories, mistakes of the past always threatening to spill into the present.

Daine was waiting for him. "Monroe, good to see you. I'd offer pleasantries but I suspect we both want to get on with business."

They shook hands. "Agreed. It's not good, Bennett. I may have stepped in the bat guano this time."

"That can wait. Joshua hasn't checked in. He was supposed to pick up Lina at the...."

"I know. That's what I have to tell you."

"You know where he is?"

"No. I wish I did. He's with her, though."

"Then they're safe, we can find them, get them home."

"I'm afraid it's not that simple. They're with Aaron Beckman."

That stunned Daine. "Beckman? What can he possibly have to do with this? He's been off the radar for what, a decade?"

"Off the legitimate radar but he's been busy. And that's how this all started."

"Then you'd better tell me."

"It began long ago. Beckman and I were brought up at the same time. I was a toe the line guy, still am but for one exception, which I'll get to. Beckman always had something going on the side, nothing the agency could put a finger on and nothing much in those days. His cover was not unlike yours, businessman looking to do some shady deals. The difference is you had a legitimate business, the company created his, funded it. Soon he liked the lifestyle and began putting away a little here and there."

He paused, gathering his thoughts. "No one really minded, almost expected in those days. If he'd stopped there, fine, but of course a black heart never can."

Bennett's look said get to the point.

"My assignment was to get Yurovinsky out of Russia, it was the Soviet Union then, so much has changed and yet sometimes I think nothing has changed."

Kellenstone waited for his reaction; surprise as he'd hoped. "He'd been needling the wrong people. His scientific skills were already known and either they'd use that for nefarious purposes or he'd be in a gulag, never to be heard from again. I contacted him to see if he was interested. He was. It was only later I found out why he was so eager."

"Out of Russia? I'd have thought that was obvious. Before *glasnost*, not an easy place and definitely not for brilliant men who challenge the system."

"Yes, you're right. And that's what I thought, at first. He was insistent that the only place he would go is if we could get him into Oxford. He'd always dreamed of Oxford. He was holding back, I could sense that and pushed for the truth. He agreed but only when he was safely out of the country. So we got him a scholarship, one of those international good will things."

"I know all that. Why would he think I had anything to do with that?"

"You were British but he held up his end, he told me you were put up for adoption by his parents, that your birth parents were executed as spies. His parents felt you would one day be under scrutiny or grow up under that cloud. They were your godparents, friends. They knew of a British couple, he working for the foreign secretary, childless and with some help - Beckman was very good with fake documents - arranged the adoption. Apparently it wasn't hard, the wife was stay at home, it was winter and she wore heavy coats, to say she had been pregnant."

Bennett tried to take this in. "But the…. other couple, didn't someone notice their baby went missing?"

"Apparently not or didn't want to know. They were in hiding, she gave birth and gave to Yurovinsky's parents to raise you as his brother."

"How does that relate to Joshua's whereabouts?"

Kellenstone nodded. "Beckman seems to have run short of funds. He had kept the original birth certificate but he wanted a copy of the fake one. Blackmail. He was coming for you. I suppose he thought you'd pay to avoid the scandal. But you're not so easy to get to, even for a man like him. He needed one on one or it wouldn't work."

"He really thought I'd pay for that? My parents are gone, what difference would it make?"

"I suspect there's more but I can't think what. It has to be why he's using Joshua to get to you." He sighed and covered his face with his hands. "It gets worse."

"Worse than holding my son for ransom? I'll pay, of course, why hasn't he asked for the money? Maybe it's not more than that."

"While he retrieved that birth certificate he found another one that was filed under the family name and yours was originally under Yurovinsky. They were to be your legal parents, and only they were aware of your birth parents circumstances. The deal was made before you were born."

His parents had early on told him he was adopted, a war orphan but as a British war orphan, they didn't know anything about his parents. He had blue eyes, they had brown and hazel, obvious enough they had to tell him something. They were gone, he couldn't verify and also knew Kellenstone would lie for any reason he deemed appropriate.

"There's more."

"Isn't there always? Yevi came to Oxford. We hit it off, I don't really remember how we met. He eventually told me about my parents, that they had been forced by circumstances to hand over to his parents, that we would be raised as brothers. He was vague about the circumstances, said it was due to rationing that his parents could not afford to feed two children. He was older, it would be more disruptive. And they knew of this couple, fine English people, who were desperate for a baby. It seemed so easy for them, to give me a better life."

"And you believed him?"

"Not at first, of course. But my parents were kind people, knew the sacrifice to give up a child so, for a few years anyway, sent photos. He showed them to me, duplicates of ones I had. And he had one grainy picture of my parents."

"Did he meet your parents?"

"A few times, when they came to visit. If they were suspicious they never let on and he had no intention of spoiling their happiness."

"Did you ever tell them?"

"No. It didn't matter that much to me, I had no memories of it. Maybe had they lived longer but they were so proud of me, I was doing well at Oxford preparing to take on the world."

"Ah yes, all those Oxford firsts. You made quite a name for yourself. You and Yurovinsky stayed close."

"Yes. But I didn't think how that would affect Yevi. Is he involved in this?"

"I don't think so, no. He seems to genuinely care for you, as a brother. But that's not the real problem."

"The tangled web of intrigue. Monroe, my son is getting out, if he won't listen to me then whatever you have to do."

"Then you won't like the next part, I'm afraid. Lina Yurovinskova is my daughter."

"How did…. Are you sure… ?" He couldn't process and walked across, to pour a drink. He drank in one gulp then turned to Kellenstone, who shook his head. Daine poured another and returned to his chair but he didn't drink.

"It was a stupid affair, a young lonely man in a foreign country, With Yurovinsky away I was to keep an eye on Sonja, her mother. She was so beautiful then. Her husband had just defected, she was frightened. He wanted me to bring her out. She refused and I tried to convince her and….. "

"And?"

"And when she contacted me, months later, she told everyone Yevi had gotten her pregnant before he left. But the math didn't work and she sent a photo, the baby looked exactly like a photo of my sister. I turned to Beckman to set up an account off the books, so she would be taken care of. My career was moving up and I was being reassigned. An illegitimate Russian child would have been the end. I thought if I sent money, it would be enough."

"But Beckman found out."

"Not at first. I just said I wanted a slush fund, for a few extras. He understood that. But when he was getting your birth certificate he saw hers and noticed the dates. He didn't connect it right away but he has a nose for these things, it's how he survives and keeps bouncing back, I suppose. He went round to talk to Sonja. She was by then more than willing to talk for a bottle." He looked ready to cry. "Lina inherited her mother's looks, Beckman couldn't resist. He was always one to play, take advantage although I guess I can't be one to speak ill of that."

"Beckman and Lina. Oh my God. Monroe, I'm…."

"Don't say it. I take full responsibility. I chose career over doing the right thing."

Bennett thought hard, had he done that? Not abandonment but through neglect? If, no, when he found his son he'd do whatever it took to win him back. He thought of his wife. Elyanna. Her grandparents had emigrated from Sweden. Her curly blond hair and deep blue eyes clashed with her slight Bronx accent; he used to tease her about that. She'd pretend to be furious but couldn't hold it and burst out laughing. He loved her laugh, it lit her up. He missed her so much, had buried so much pain. No wonder his son hated him, how much pain had he been forced to bury because they never talked about it. Time to be a man, how many times had he told him that?

Bennett Daine was a wealthy man but he couldn't turn back time. He began to wonder what was the value of money if all it bought was big houses, private planes and people to do your bidding. Money made life easier, to be sure, but it couldn't bring about what mattered most.

"Does Yevi know? About Lina?"

"I don't think so. He wanted to return after Oxford but it was too risky for another return, he'd barely gotten out that time. The country was in changing, no way to know how it would turn out. I think we both failed her because as his career took off his pleas to get his family out were less frequent."

"Until a man wants to make peace with his past."

Both men sat, lost in their respective thoughts of loss and failure when Valerie and Rod burst through the door.

Valerie didn't say hello. "Where was your house in Stockholm? The address?"

Bennett looked confused. "What house? I've never lived in Stockholm. I stay at the embassy."

She looked at Rod. She was too emotional to speak, he took over.

"We've been to see the Russian. He's heavily sedated and prognosis bleak. But we managed to ask him a question, where might Lina take Joshua if they haven't left the country by boat. He said you lived in a house when you were a boy. He bought it for you, as a surprise."

"He must be delirious. We lived in North London."

Monroe spoke. "No. Wait. I didn't pay much attention but when your father was with the foreign service office he was stationed here for several years before returning to London. I suppose when you were at school age."

"I had no idea. Do you know the address?"

"Not listed that I remember."

It took mere seconds before all spoke at once.

"Records office!"

Monroe took out his phone. He called Midget, she'd find it, bloodhound that she was and no one would know.

Nearly an hour later when all but Rod were ready to charge out the door in any direction just to do something, Bernmeister did his job and kept everyone on point. Daine and Kellenstone had brought the other two up to speed.

"Once we find this house then what? Beckman has no doubt planned it, knowing we'd find it eventually. Even if Yurovinsky dies and he may not know his condition, alive or dead, but Lina would insist he check. The doctor has orders to forward any calls to Nigel so as of now it's possible he doesn't know. Unless that guard dog of his is somehow tied in."

"He looked genuinely concerned," Valerie said.

"I agree. But we can't assume anything."

"We need a plan."

Daine and Kellenstone looked at him. He gave minimal thought to his two kids, his wife had said it was better if her new husband adopted them, he was a stranger to them by then, and his siblings were doing fine without him. But he saw in the two men's eyes the fear for their offspring, even though grown. He'd long ago vowed to never love anyone again, the loss wasn't worth it.

"Beckman knows what all of you look like but I doubt he would recognize me. I'll put on the sports jersey and scope out the neighborhood. Somebody check, see if the team played today, I can use that."

"We can use that. He's my partner. I rescue him."

Daine nodded, Bernmeister shrugged. She left the room to change.

Kellenstone had Midget check old personnel files, within minutes she called with the address. "We've got it all. Go." Rod and Valerie left.

Daine said, "It's still not clear how Beckman knew of the plan change. Joshua said it was an ambush."

Kellenstone sighed. "That's on me. I knew Gallagher was ambitious. She wasn't my choice for second in command, pushed on me by someone close to the administration. I knew she was there to keep them informed of my whereabouts. In their eyes I was slipping off the reservation, too many secrets and not the national security kind. I began to suspect Beckman was being paid off the books. I told her as little as possible but she's clever, couldn't keep her out of all loops. She could have learned of the location swap but honestly, I didn't think she'd be that fast. I felt the first one had been compromised."

He shook his head. "I don't yet know why she became a liability other than he doesn't like loose ends. We traced her last incoming call to a nearby cell tower but no listed number. It's already buried as a random attack. I like to think she wasn't yet fully committed to the dark side, that she believed she was doing the right thing. When she picked up Valerie, on my orders, your son had been reported dead. She thought she was bringing a valued asset home. That put her right in the middle of it."

Daine was pacing, edgy. In business he had learned patience, watching currency values drop when others bailed, quietly focused, sensing the market would fall further thereby as much as doubling profits. But knowing where his son was yet unable to act while others took over was akin to his long ago helplessness during his wife's illness.

He almost didn't hear when Monroe spoke. "Pour that drink for me, Bennett. One more thing."

What now? Carefully, hands unsteady, he poured a large shot for each, handed it over and waited.

"I've saved the worst for last. Beckman is working with Lina's husband. The proof, from a reliable source long ago planted in the government, is on the computer drive. He could only get it to the Czech Republic, too risky otherwise. Your son and his partner are the best at retrieval, they were nearby, so I figured nothing would go wrong. Enough evidence to finally charge Beckman, too good to pass up."

"Could it all have been a setup? From the beginning?"

Kellenstone thought a minute. "Anything is possible. He wasn't supposed to know that source, put in place before suspicions of him grew. But this new team, long in the planning, yes, it's possible. I've become a fossil, Bennett, there was a time I'd have been less anxious to jump on it."

"We were arrogant enough to think we had all the answers. Meanwhile, they were rebuilding. Using terrorism as a blind."

"Beckman planned to kill Yurovinsky, that speech could ruin his financial arrangements. By using LIna as bait, he saw an opening to get to you. Turning off lights let him or her get away but hardly optimum aim. Don't look at me like that. If the professor was dead you would have told me."

"But why? After all this time, why Yevi? He's been preaching the same song for years."

"Look around. Kids protesting. UN reports. Wacky weather. Global warming has gone mainstream. Specifically, as international laws to curtail carbon emissions get onto agendas it could decimate the Russian oil fields. Ours, too, a top donor to this administration is heavily into energy production, would ruin him, he's paid millions, to loosen regulations. Yurovinsky had a plan to unite all the groups, under one banner, they would become far more potent."

He sipped his drink. "It's always about money."

#   #

Chapter 14

Joshua, still in his guard's uniform, was unhappy for a variety of reasons. For one, he was tied up, Beckman had used wet leather strips pulled taut that, as they dried, would bite into his skin. For another, he was standing on a chair, rope around his neck and wrapped around a ceiling fan so that if he struggled to loosen the ties and tipped the chair he would likely hang himself. The ceiling fan was old, the ceiling cracked in a few places and his weight might rip it out but not necessarily in time to regain oxygen and survive.

Odds were bad, for sure, but what really brought down his mood were the sounds coming from the bedroom. Beckman hadn't closed the door all the way, no doubt he enjoyed starring in his own perverted reality show. Joshua had never thought of sex as a spectator sport and the grunts and groans, mostly from Lina although a few suggested that Beckman needed a little help in that department. Way too many minutes of hard breathing later, Lina screeched with delight and then silence.

If he'd hoped for a post coital slumber to better assess his situation he was out of luck. Beckman strolled out, in undershorts, his bony legs and sagging chest skin in contrast to his surgery enhanced face, grotesque in the lessening daylight. The Bowie knife, even now, was strapped at his waist, a striking metaphor to male enhancement. It was a visual that was likely to burn in his brain forever.

"Ah, Joshua, still here, I see. Are those too tight, yet? No? Soon enough you won't be able to resist the struggle to loosen them. But leather tied when wet eventually cuts off circulation. In the right places it can slowly kill. A little trick I picked up in 'Nam."

"You weren't in 'Nam. A year too young according to your official bio. Except it's not true, you just dodged the draft."

"Didn't have to go, did my bit, infiltrated protesters. Met some guys in a bar, drinkin', couldn't tell me enough stories about how much money to be made after war, black markets, government contracts, easy as pickin' apples off a tree. And a few tricks to keep the natives in line while they continued to rape the country. Black ops, more my line."

"It must have sounded like a war just made for you, kindred spirits and all. Ever think they were pulling your leg, gullible kid they probably saw in you."

"Fuck with me all you want, you pansy rich boy. I'm not the one tied to a light fixture." Beckman did not like anyone fucking with his self-created image.

"What are your plans? If you wanted me dead, I suspect I'd be dead."

"Too smart for your own good, always were. Like she said, I want that computer drive. It has information I can use. Someone tried to sell me out and I can't let that pass. Then I need to find myself a nice little island somewhere safe, live out my days in peace, find me a good woman, like your partner maybe."

Joshua went cold but said nothing.

"Oh, don't worry, she's too complicated for me. Take Lina, for instance. All she wants is money. She likes being rich more than anyone I've ever known. Even me. I like it's convenience, sure, but she inhales it. For that, she'll do anything."

"Where does my father fit in? He can set you up, all you have to do is ask."

"Oh, I plan to. Fair trade. But there's more, scores to settle, jobs to do."

"Such as?"

"In due time we'll get to that but for now I'm going out. Don't waste your time thinking about Lina. She's out for the duration, a little something in her drink. Like her mother, just another drunk."

Joshua held on to every ounce of control he had to not kick him in the teeth. And thereby hang himself.

Beckman took a step back, as if realized his prey was more dangerous than thought. He returned to the bedroom, soon the shower sounds replaced Lina's light snoring.

An hour later, Beckman gone, Joshua was uncomfortable but had used the time to think. Beckman had a plan, it included his father and maybe Valerie, but why? What was behind his coming out of hiding? He'd always bounced back into someone's good graces, always war mongers to pay his freight, cover up his side businesses. None of that was a secret. Yet here he was, after something and willing to risk everything to that end. The information they'd gotten out of the embassy? Beckman had connections, likely could have quashed whatever was on it. Or at least been paid enough to go away and let it disappear, save the company embarrassment, common governmental exit strategy. Hide the damaging secrets.

He heard stirrings from the other room. Beckman could be anywhere from a bar picking up women to building and stashing explosives, no idea how long he'd be gone. Wherever he was, no good would come of it. He was pretty sure Valerie was nearby, whether he could sense it or just knew her choices he wasn't sure. She would have gotten his note and be waiting for contact, when it didn't come she'd get a little crazy but somehow figure it out. His father was either with Yevi or Valerie and that meant Rod, too.

Joshua had mixed feelings about Bernmeister. He kept a lot to himself so you never knew what he was thinking. Yet he believed the soldier's loyalty to his father was absolute. After that was anyone's guess.

Lina was mumbling in her sleep and from sounds, tossing and turning. Would she help or hurt his situation? If she staggered out she could stumble into the chair. Even if he could grab her she didn't weight much. His legs were left untied, Beckman probably figured he'd use them to try to wrest free and it would backfire. Not the best plan but under the circumstances it might have to do. Waiting for Beckman's return was far worse. He was prepared to kill, with or without the information he wanted.

Was that even what this was about? Beckman was pure evil, as few are, most do evil things for a misguided purpose or illness. It was possible he was tired of hiding, the loss of powerful people that feared him. Maybe he just wanted to remind everyone who he was.

Like they didn't already know but too often dismissed. Ignore evil and it doesn't go away; it may hibernate but will return stronger just as an ill wind becomes a gale force of destruction.

He heard Lina stagger into the bathroom. This was like prison, you can hear but can't see, far worse to the senses. His ties had begun to shrink, soon it would be a real problem. If he could get her to wet them maybe he could stretch enough to break free. He thought a minute. She wasn't fully awake but maybe he could get her attention.

"Lina. Come out here. I have a question."

It took a full four minutes for her to stagger out, in a long tee, be grateful for small favors, he thought. "Before your man kills me I need to know something."

"Hmph. Whassat?"

"Why did you refuse to marry me?" Her ego would step up to block out that it was the other way around.

She stared at him, confused. "Why did I?"

"Our fathers thought we would grow up and marry. Why didn't we?"

"Because my mother said he was not my real father. My father was American. He sent money. You were my brother."

That stunned him. Was she telling the truth or too confused to know what she was saying? But now wasn't the time to dwell on that, he had to get untied.

"If you do me a favor we can talk about my father. He's left everything to me and that's not fair if you're my sister."

"I am your sister! I should get half." How easy to swallow a lie when money's attached.

"That's what I said. Give me a phone, I'll call him and tell him."

"Why are you standing like that?"

"If you bring me some water I'll tell you."

"Aaron would not like that."

"He's going to kill us both when he returns. I heard him talking."

"No, you're lying. He loves me."

"He put something in your drink, look at you. You're not sleepy, you're drugged. He said you can't travel with him. He's going off the grid and you can't live like that."

"Because I am a lady."

Yeah, sure, whatever. "Bring me a glass of water. Loosen my ties. You don't have to untie them. He's gone, another woman. I heard her voice over the phone."

"You're lying." She started to cry. "He wouldn't do that. He's taking me to America. He has a mansion all ready for me."

"No, he doesn't. He can't return, he'll be arrested. He's using me to get money from my father - our father - so he can hide. That's half your money, too."

"Half?"

"Somewhere far away, in Asia, he said."

"Asia?"

Patience. "Yes, he has a place in the mountains, no indoor plumbing but he's a handy guy, can probably arrange something."

She collapsed on the sofa. A spring bounced up. "What do I do? My husband…"

"If you help me, I'll say after the shots you went into hiding, with me, for your safety."

She thought this over then smiled. "Yes. My father was stopped from saying his name. He will keep his oil rights, we will still be rich." She was starting to sag.

Quickly, he said, "Richer than before. He will be a hero for stopping the conference. He will be rewarded. Your president loves to reward his loyal followers."

"Yes. He does. You will come with me?"

"Of course I will. We're family." Whatever.

She staggered in the kitchen. Joshua wished she'd hurry, before Beckman returned. He heard a car coming down the street, this late there was not much traffic.

The car passed. Noises from the kitchen, how long did it take to fill a glass with water? He was not in a position to rush her.

She returned, unsure why but a full glass in her hand.

"Lina. Listen carefully, this is important." She blinked and stared, blank eyed at him. "Walk around behind me and pour the water on my wrist. The ties are too tight, it will make them more comfortable." She continued staring. "For our plans. I can't call my father if I can't reach the phone."

She nodded and finally moved around behind him.

"Now pour the water slowly over the ties. No, don't touch me. That's it, good girl. Aaron always said you helped him. I'll explain how you helped and he will find a place to live that you can visit. Your own mansion. He will soon be really rich. That's right, keep pouring, all around to keep them wet, very important to do it just right."

"I'm tired. I want to sleep."

"Yes, you should do that. Rest up before Aaron returns, look your best."

She shuffled from the room.

Slowly, so as to not upend the chair, he gradually loosened the leather strips. It was tricky since they'd been put on wet and tight. He had to stretch them further. But Beckman, in a hurry, hadn't pulled fully, one quick yank. Now he found he could ease one out further. Slow going since he couldn't twist or risk a sudden movement. Finally, he was able to stretch enough to make a fist, just in time as Beckman appeared.

He'd made no sound, yet there he was. Only a sliver of light from the kitchen window showed it was a person not a shadow. It startled Joshua although he didn't move, hoping he hadn't been there long. He could kick out but if the ceiling fan didn't collapse, he would. Hopefully, the darkness behind him hid the water on the floor.

Beckman, true to form, couldn't help but brag. "I've set a trap for your father, let him know where you are. Frankly, I'm disappointed. I thought he'd figure out the address long before this. He's slipping."

Keep him talking. "Are you sure? How about Kellenstone, where is he in all this?"

"Don't make me laugh. He's only still there to deflect the real opportunities out there. Go on the talk shows, a front man of legitimacy." He laughed at his self-perceived brilliance.

"You ever going to share your plan? Not seeing that sharp hawkish mind you're so famous for. Probably just a myth anyway. You were always good at blasting your own horn for all to hear but maybe results a little trickier to calculate."

He stepped forward, stuck the cold muzzle of Joshua's gun to his stomach.

"You really don't want to piss me off. For now I can use you but that can change."

Rustling sounds from the bedroom and Lina appeared in the doorway. "Aaron, he said you were leaving without me. But I don't care. I will buy my own mansion in America. I will be a Daine, Lina Daine. Uncle Bennett is really my father. Did you know that?"

Oh shit, thought Joshua. This could go bad fast. He had one hand almost out of the straps but couldn't risk any movement.

"That's really nice to know. Why don't you stand there, next to him, so I can see the resemblance. Maybe you two can put on a show for me before I shoot you both." He cackled with delight.

"I don't like you anymore. I will find someone younger, someone who can perform without so much help."

Never one for discretion, drugged she had no filter or apparently any sense, thought Joshua. But she'd stepped in front of him. Calculating his odds it was probably now or never.

He yanked his hands free, grabbed her and pulled her up then jumped sideways so their bodies acted as ballast. With a huge crash the ceiling fan came tumbling down. He twisted so the blades only brushed his shoulder, painful but no real damage. Lina was not so lucky; she screamed, flailing. She was on top of him and he was forced to shield from the blows, not because it hurt but to slide her off.

Beckman jumped backwards and fired simultaneously at where he'd been tied. The bullet lodged high in the wall. Lina started screaming. Whether Beckman meant to shoot Joshua, anticipating where he'd be on the floor or chose to silence her, the next bullet went right through her heart, missing Joshua by an inch. He slid out from under her, grabbed the fan, swung sideways and sent the flying trajectile to the gun's flash. Beckman raised his arm to fend off the blow and swore as it struck him. The gun fell to the floor.

Not his knife hand however, as he pulled it out, swinging madly. Light reflected off the steel and Joshua, a little slow for having been unable to move for several hours, still easily deflected although it nicked his shoulder.

"You won't win this fight, Daine, not with my Bessie girl here."

A knife with a name. The guy was born a century late. Hoping to rile him, he said, "You forget, Beckman, you're not up to speed either."

He was manic, slicing the air wildly. Joshua still had a fan blade to block but the old guy was quick, clearly on something, no doubt where he went, to the friendly neighborhood cocaine dealer.

But it would soon wear off. Keep him moving, circling around.

Just then the sound of another gunshot, at the front door. Then a loud crack as the rotting hinges gave way and it flew open.

Valerie and Rod burst through. Beckman, outnumbered, ran out the back.

Valerie yelled, "I've got this." And headed after him.

Joshua said, "No. He's mine. Stay here, take care of her," and ran, ahead of her. She watched him go, debating orders versus…. oh hell, no, and off she went.

Rod, with all the emotion of someone checking a grocery list, took out his phone.

"Sir, we have a situation."

The land of the midnight sun had finally decided to call it a day and a half moon showed Beckman or at least a moving shadow up ahead, running low, almost tripping. Joshua easily gained on the older man as he headed for the small pier, aligned with many colorful crafts where he'd left a small motor boat prepared for a quick getaway. He clamored in, pulled the cord and as it roared to life, headed out into the channel just as Joshua arrived, seconds too late. He dove in the water, ignoring the chill, and swam towards the boat. Beckman sensed more than saw and began to zig zag but he had to steer and as his pursuer gained, he grabbed a spare gas can to use as a weapon.

Joshua grabbed the side, easily deflected and began to climb in. Beckman tried to swerve around so the propellers would end him. But he hung on and swung with it. Beckman grabbed his knife but in doing so let go of the wheel. Joshua took the opportunity for a hefty downward push down on the rim.

Beckman tried to lunge with the knife but lost his balance and fell sideways. Joshua yanked his arm and pounded down on the metal siding. Beckman yelled in pain yet kept his grip but his arm was damaged and three slams later his arm disabled enough that the knife dropped into the water.

He reacted as if his arm had gone overboard. Automatically he dove in after it. Joshua clamored into the boat but the swaying movement caused him to stumble, briefly off balance. He regained footing and but realized swimming was faster and dove in after the fleeing man, swimming for the opposite shore.

Valerie arrived at water's edge. She had heard not seen the splashes, calculated what had happened and waded out for the boat tow, careful to not get sucked under as it motored aimlessly, to rescue her partner. She upended in and carefully steered into the inky water as she searched for any sign; neither were visible on the calm surface. She didn't want to risk driving over Joshua and stayed far enough back.

Beckman was a surprisingly strong swimmer and underwater swam towards the *Pålsundsbron* or Western Bridge. Joshua, a better swimmer but unable to see far ahead, had no idea which direction to go. He surfaced, saw a ripple, dove back under.

The glint of moonlight was enough for Valerie, she saw the dive. She drove carefully so as to not slice with the propeller.

Joshua surfaced to catch his breath. "Did you see him?"

"Nothing. At least an hour to daylight, he could be hiding anywhere." The channel had pilings and walkways and boats tied to shore, a million places to hide in the dark. Waiting for the light, however, and he could be far away, never to be seen again.

He lifted one leg over, gently rocking the boat forcing her to shift her balance as he deftly slid in, splashing her. She didn't notice.

He studied the area as his eyes adjusted. "The bridge. He'll reach the bridge. Over to *Langholmen*, crawl along the viaduct, disappear. We've got to find him. Anyone on the docks at daybreak, he'll kill and take their boat. If he manages that...."

Less concerned now with the propeller she roared the engine to life and headed for the bridge. She found the boat's high beam light switch and they began to sweep the surface for any movement.

"Wait. Over there, something moved." She shone the light across. "There he is. Pull to shore, I can make faster time on the bridge, meet him at the other side."

She maneuvered close to the bridge piling as he jumped out and up the bank, slipping once, onto the bridge.

Beckman could hear the motor as it neared shore, could guess there would be footsteps above him. He quickly changed direction. He could swim the channel, there were markers left from when boats were stopped for tolls. Once on the island he would find shelter; with daylight soon he had to hurry. He would kill that son of a bitch, he should have done it at the house but that stupid little bitch insisted he would give her the information he wanted. Women had always been his downfall but killing her was symbolic, he'd already decided he'd had enough raw meat as he'd often bragged was his for the taking.

Such enlightenment came too late. Joshua saw him shift direction and rather than meet him at the other end, a risk it might throw an advantage, he climbed over the low wall, down the arched supports and dove in the water. It was less than a high dive, which he'd loved as a kid while his friends at school watched, in awe. It was the beginning of his risk taking, attention he craved.

It was a nearly clean dive, too late he worried about depth but managed to twist upright in plenty of time. Beckman was almost to shore but he must be tiring, not in the shape he once was and as his drugs wore off he began to falter. Joshua easily caught up, reached out to grab him but the water made him slippery. He took the opening and kicked hard, connected with some body part just as he touched land. Futilely, he began to crawl up the grassy bank. Joshua grabbed again, more firmly. Beckman kicked again but this time he was ready for him and held on to his foot, as he struggled unsuccessfully.

Aaron Beckman was no match for Joshua Daine.

The barest glimmer of a new spring day hinted at the gorgeous Stockholm skyline. Valerie stood in the boat, hands held high. Then had to quickly stoop to grab the side or risk a briskly cold swim. She quickly steered across the channel so that Joshua could dump in the nearly drowned Beckman and deftly brought the three river rats back to the opposite shore.

Bernmeister watched as Joshua almost threw Beckman on land, letting him stumble and made no effort to help Valerie out of the rocking boat as she tied it up. Instead he had found the leather ties, knew exactly what they were and dipped them in the salt water from the sea, knowing that would hurt all the more.

He helped Joshua haul up the exhausted and furious Beckman. He was still struggling more from ire than strength and while it probably didn't take both of them it was done in record time. He attached the ties firmly to Beckman's wrists. Each man grabbed a shoulder and dragged him up the incline. Valerie followed, unneeded, not at all pleased.

Inside the small house Bennett stood alone, anxiously waiting, visibly relieved when he heard sounds from the waterfront. Across the room Monroe was given a few moments to grieve the daughter he'd never known. When the bedraggled foursome entered through the kitchen door he ignored all but Joshua and latched on to his muddy dripping son in a hug long overdue and held on way too long, unwilling to let go. Bernmeister shoved an even more disheveled Beckman onto the dank sofa. Drained of all fight he remained where he lay, awkwardly half on, legs over.

Joshua, enveloped by his father, didn't move, unsure how he felt. Valerie watched, again realized her irrelevance. If any thoughts of her own father passed through, she remained expressionless.

Bernmeister saw a message on his phone, to call Nigel.

He listened a minute, then said,"Sir?"

Bennett released his son, to his relief, and turned.

"The professor, sir. He's unlikely to last much longer."

"Let's go." He turned to his son. He started to say something then nodded and walked out with Rod.

Joshua turned to Valerie. "This place could use some sprucing up, nice little vacation home."

229

She stared at him. Maybe his brain was waterlogged. He pulled her aside. "Stay with Monroe. Get him gone, plausible denial. He can't be anywhere near this. Make him listen. I'll take care of cleanup here. Find out what happened."

She had a thousand questions but now wasn't the time. She nodded.

"I almost forgot. We still have this." She pulled out the computer stick, still in it's plastic bag, hoping it hadn't gotten wet. She nodded towards Kellenstone. "It's his, you know, that was the assignment."

"I sure hope it was worth all the trouble." He gently touched Kellenstone's arm. "Sir. I believe this belongs to you."

He took the tiny package, nodded.

"I need you to leave. Now. There are things to be done and you can't be part of it. I'm sorry."

Company man to the end he glanced once more at the child he never knew and left with Valerie.

Joshua called his friend Johannes and told him he was about to earn enough to retire forever. He explained what he needed. Behind him, like an unused rag doll, the drugs worn off, Beckman continued to babble incoherently but appeared to be unconscious. To be sure, though, Joshua made sure his ties were tight enough, circulation be damned.

He stared down at Beckman, a man who had talked weak presidents into wars, whose greed allowed laundered drug money safe passage, who had killed Lina in cold blood and how many others not known.

He could easily put a bullet in the man's head, spare the world. Watching Kellenstone, though, it was clear he was the American father, not his own. Beckman was his to kill, he would not take that away.

#   #

Chapter 15

To Bennett the drive to the clinic located off the road in a nondescript industrial area before *Malmö*, was nearly two hours and seemed forever. He forced himself to empty his mind, to think about what he wanted to say. When he arrived, though, Yevi was gone. Bennett stared at his lifelong friend, had he done enough for him?

Dr. Fassbinder was nervous, he now had a dead body he hadn't reported. Bernmeister explained he could now do that, he had treated the wound and prepared the paperwork as required but then had to monitor through the night. All was in order. Olaf would explain the circumstances, coordinate his return home. There would be no trouble.

Nigel handed over a tape recorder to Rod. It was an older model, Buck had it for backup to the doctor's recorder. He could take it, they'd ordered a new one.

Bennett waited until they'd returned to the safe house to listen, privately. Nigel went out for food and he and Rod caught up over a feast, relaxing as they so rarely could.

"Bennett, my best friend and brother." His voice was weak, barely recognizable. "I am not long, I know that. And I know you will take care of my Lina. I wish I had been there for her. I have to tell you what I should have told you long ago. So much shame. Your parents, I told you your parents died. I did not tell you they were executed as traitors. That part was true. What was not true is they betrayed their country. My parents turned them in, to save themselves. That's why they let you be adopted. To look at you, to know what they did….."

A long pause. He could hear Olaf's voice calling the doctor. "No, there is no time," his voice to someone, a whisper. After a few moments, he began again, "I left papers, at my home, there was a loose stone in the fireplace. I hid them and sealed it up. Your real name and birth certificate. It may be too late, for both of us. But our children, for them…."

Now Olaf's voice was louder, calling the doctor. No one thought to turn off the recorder until the doctor pronounced his lifelong friend dead at 8:52 a.m.

Bennett stared out the window for a long time, trying to absorb what it all meant. Was it too late? If he were honest he'd not thought much of his birth parents over the years and he had no memory at all. His adoptive parents were good to him, dedicated to giving him the best they could afford. A foreign service officer was never rich but his mother was loving and a fine cook. She gardened and her flowers were the envy of neighbors. He'd been happy. His success came from some inner drive, unquestioned by him.

Perhaps that's why the loss of Elyanna had cut him off from his emotions. His father had died from a heart attack his last year at Oxford. He'd never gotten to say goodbye, he was too busy to grieve much and maybe had neglected his mother as he began his life. She was supportive, always, of him but she, too, died relatively young. He'd been with her at the end, to tell her she gave him a wonderful life, he'd been a happy child. She'd told him the first time she had held him she knew it was the right thing and how much she loved him.

His wife had tried to tell his son the same but he was still a boy, he didn't understand death or why the world he knew had left. Bennett had known loss but never such a gut wrenching dissolution of everything he felt and he could not conquer his own grief even for his son. For the first time he saw himself through his son's eyes and did not like what he knew to be true. Was it too late? He had no idea but he had to try.

He would make arrangements to bring Yevi's body to Oxford and a funeral. He had been well liked by most of his colleagues, the other dons, he was prickly but could be great fun, and generous. They would drink to his work and he would set up a foundation to further his progress, to fund others who would follow in his footsteps. He would recover the hidden papers, his birthright, and decide what to do.

Sadly, or maybe for the best, he knew Lina would have to be cremated, whereabouts unknown. His son would see to cleanup and that, to him, was also sad. But he'd made his fortune by negotiating, whatever it took he would see that his son came home. Too many demons would destroy him. It was not yet too late.

# #

Valerie allowed Kellenstone the lead in his disappearance. Obviously because he was her superior but also it's what he'd done most of his professional life. Someone named Midget was at his beck and call. Apparently the office next to Missy was for show, he had another more secret workplace. He asked her to drive, no where in particular, as he stared out the window between phone calls that consisted, on his part at least, mostly of grunts. Just as she was wondering if he'd lost touch he told her to drop him on some nondescript street corner.

He directed her through unfamiliar back streets and narrow lanes, where she was barely able to squeeze through the parked cars. Finally, after a turn that missed losing a bumper by a skinny finger, he barked, "Here." Presumably that meant stop, in the middle of a block of tall buildings, old enough for Vikings to have inhabited, she fumed to herself. He lumbered out, took two steps before he remembered how he got there.

"Thank you, Valerie. You've done good work. I'm sorry for what we put you through but considering the results I think you'll understand it was necessary."

"Yes sir."

She watched as a battered car drove up and he got in. Her instinct was to jump out after but nothing about him seemed to scream panic. He'd always said the more you look forgettable the longer your life as field agents will be. He'd said that at one of her training lectures. Not odd that she remembered it now, while she spent five minutes trying to back out of the awkward spot. Two teenagers up ahead stopped kissing to watch her, laughing. She wanted to thrust out her middle finger but the steering wheel took both hands.

For a brief moment she felt irrelevant, her job completed, no idea about, or if, a new assignment, what was she to any of them? Being forgettable was fine in the field but not so much when left behind.

She'd spent time here over the years, it was a good anchor city for and between assignments, safe and fun, things to do but privacy also. Once she had fancied buying a small boat so she could sail out and feel completely alone in the universe but soon realized it was a boat crazed city, she'd need a blindfold to avoid sightseers gliding through the gentle waters and locals out for some air after winter sports season ended and holiday spirits greeted spring.

Midsummer, in late June, when it all burst through in a huge block party spanning a dozen or more islands wasn't that far off. Maybe she'd stay awhile. People watching was great entertainment. After a long winter ended bringing eighteen hours of daylight, the populace let loose in an explosion of joyous dancing and drinking.

Back on a main drag she became aware of her less than forgettable attire, the dried mud and sea water were starting to itch. Since there was no message on her phone she was completely free of restraints as perhaps she'd never felt in her life.

Maybe it was time for some changes in her life. Suddenly she wanted to be alone, with these new thoughts. She wasn't sure who was at the safe house and she wasn't up to facing Bernmeister with his judgey non-expression and Mr. Daine, whom she barely knew. The Berns Hotel was still booked for another night, she'd pick up some new clothes on the way.

More than a while later, having happily spent hours with a helpful salesclerk who didn't blink at her appearance, a dirty soccer team shirt was probably a common sight, she was a completely overhauled into a new woman. Immediately sussing the situation, the sales associate, Famke, as it said on her name tag, helped Valerie find several outfits that worked with her coloring, apparently important, and fit her perfectly. Famke insisted that new under garments would change her life and to always complete an outfit with proper shoes, which she of course provided. No female should face the world without at least blush, mascara and lipstick and lucky for her a local brand was having a special. By then Valerie was putty in her hands, agreeing to a bracelet, just for fun. Also, for good measure, the name of a local hairdresser, her sister.

The sales clerk's full name was Famke Andersson, a good Swedish woman with two kids and a boring but decent husband named Hugo. He watched their kids while she went to night school, to study design. Valerie realized she hadn't had such fun with a woman since her days roaming Paris with Juliette but back then it was dampened by recent events that had left her emotionally paralyzed.

At the Berns Hotel, in an unfamiliar but exceptionally cheery mood, she swung open the door only to drop everything on the floor. On the bed, reading, looking every inch the rich playboy he often portrayed and probably was, sat her partner. Cleaned up, in a seriously expensive outfit, his shoes alone were probably double what she'd just spent. The new, not improved in her mind, Joshua Daine, heir to the Daine fortune, a class to which she'd never belonged, looked at her like she was some cat he'd dragged out of the lake.

The towels on the balcony were gone, no doubt sent to the dry cleaners by a maid.

So much for that good mood.

"Make yourself at home. Don't mind me."

He didn't move, instead she felt he could see right through her.

"I need a shower. Maybe you can find somewhere to be."

"That's two different things. Stay or go."

"Now you're an English professor?"

"I came to say thank you for coming to rescue me."

She had no idea why that irritated her. "It's what partners do. So okay, you're welcome."

"You showed up." He smiled, as happy as he'd ever been that she was safe, a realization that this time it had cut too close.

She wasn't sure what to make of that. "All in a day's work, leaving a dead body and a disgraced N.S.A. chief with a broken wrist on the floor. Not to mention a missing ceiling. Sure, no problem. I'll just follow you around with a dustbin and mop."

There was a knock on the door. Outside, a voice, "Room service."

He got off the bed. "I've got this. Take your shower. I'll be on the balcony."

She was torn. She didn't like him thinking he could just take over but she was hungry and also had two places she desperately wanted to scratch.

She took her time, washed and dried her hair, unsure of her thoughts until she tried on the light blue flowered sleeveless dress and navy sandals. Next, makeup. She'd worn it plenty of times, on assignment but that felt like playing a part. Now she was creating her own look as Famke had insisted she must have. She really did feel like a new woman.

Just before heading out, though, it occurred to her to check her phone and as suspected it had a tracker. He hadn't stumbled onto her, he knew exactly where she'd be. With very mixed feelings she opened the door.

Showing no signs of impatience he turned, the sky a backlight. Tall, ocean blue eyes drilling down, clean shaven, looking better than any man had a right to look, really pissed her off. He was her partner, he should know better.

The small table was set for two. "Sit down. We should talk."

#   #

Chapter 16

Six months later Monroe Kellenstone had returned to home base, given all the details to Midget to write up properly,which meant leaving out a few salient details. It was partially the secret to their success. No lies but occasional omissions, the main one being in this case that before he'd left Stockholm he had talked to the founder of the Global Economic and Environmental Protection Institute, Lars-Villig Birskstraach. Olaf Langsston had called him about Yurovinsky's passing, a great man gone.

But why, asked Birkstraach? Kellenstone knew why. He'd gone down to the graveyard, where old computers were kept, alone, to read the encrypted files sent by a long ago contact, still quietly on the payroll as he rose through government ranks.

The files were definitely juicy. It was proof that Beckman was being used, although knowing him it didn't take much persuasion, as a catalyst to start a drumbeat for war by this administration. The public was tired of unending skirmishes and needed prodding. A war would change the narrative, desperately needed by recent scandals in the gulping of public trough money by public officials.

Instead, he and Birkstraach had a long discussion about the future of the movement. Birkstraach, somewhat reluctantly, handed over the papers dropped by Doktor Yurovinsky he'd found on the floor realizing that in the wrong hands many more people might be harmed. He did not want that on his conscience.

Kellenstone had also seen to custody arrangements of Aaron Beckman. Kellenstone had too many emotions about his part in Lina's life to sort them out quickly with so much to be done. He'd left her to a mother, a drunk who had used the money for herself, no wonder the girl had felt so much need. He could at least keep her name out of the official record. And, if he were honest, his part in it.

Beckman, however, could not be kept off the record, the news was too great, it would leak. And so Beckman was released after he began to name names. A trial would offer up so much damaging information on so many power players that more than the Russian economy would crash. Politicians, beholden to big money interests would kill it anyway, no good would come from letting staff in on the depths of depravity around them. They needed to believe in the system to do their work. And so, recognizing that the greater good as it was pounded into those that questioned and facing reality as he often had but seldom with such distaste, Kellenstone had signed off on releasing Beckman into the wild. He would disappear as he always had, set up new operations likely more blatant because he felt protected. Or maybe he was just older, let them try to stop him, he'd just proved he was invincible. Get enough dirt on your opponents and you own them.

Kellenstone put a team on him, stay back, do nothing, just report. I want to know who he meets with, who he does business with. But Beckman soon learned his money laundering bankers wanted nothing to do with him, he was red hot to regulators. The only option now open to him was child pornography, trafficking in minors, refugees agreeing for a few pennies on the dollar, to look the other way, survival at a premium. That, to Monroe, was unacceptable.

He still had contacts and let it be known that Beckman was released after providing names of his co-conspirators. One night, late, as he left a palace of ill repute, one of the most depraved in Bangkok, he was shot in the head, twice. In that part of the city no one interfered, one more missing person. Days later, his mangled body was found just off a popular tourist gathering, his genitals were cut off, a calling card of a local gang, his Bowie knife long gone. Some wondered if without that around his waist he was lessened. The thugs happily took credit, striking fear in others who might think payment was not necessary to do business. They could be shut down later, in diplomatic negotiations.

He also had paid a visit to Melissa Gallagher's parents. He knew she'd been double dealing, a plant from someone in the administration, he wasn't entirely sure as more than a few wanted him derailed. Not so easy they'd found and while she was ambitious and anxious to replace him she must have balked at being used. She had called him, asking to speak privately, off the record, it was important. Unfortunately, he was knee deep in retrieving the Beckman info and put her off. They would sense a change in her, maybe a tapped phone, and as leverage would set up a fake account in her name to keep her in line; that she apparently knew nothing about it meant she had become a liability. She'd paid the ultimate price for finally stepping up or at least that's how he preferred to think of her. He would tell her parents she had died serving her country with honor. He wasn't entirely sure of that but he was sure it was what they wanted to hear.

Two weeks later Monroe Kellenstone suffered a mild heart attack and turned in his papers. He smiled through the toasts and jokes before he disappeared to a little cabin by a river in Illinois, not far from where he'd grown up. His nephews were grown, had kids of their own and all were welcome, fishing was great in the spring.

Midget moved in with her youngest son as part time babysitter. Four boys. Exactly right in her mind. Once a year they all packed up to visit Uncle Monroe.

None of his neighbors knew that he'd spent his entire adult life working to keep America safe. In today's world that wasn't easy, maybe it never had been but the current disruptive administration was on the way out, kicking and screaming. He had hope that the country he'd worked so hard to protect was on the right track but it was up to others now.

The computer drive that had so many months ago put everything in motion, that had the proof of Aaron Beckman's many crimes, had disappeared. No matter, the information on it was no longer important.

One final act. He dropped two envelopes in a mailbox, addressed to the New York Times and the Washington Post, that contained the names and financial disclosures that Yevgeny Yurovinsky was

244

going to announce from the podium. The incoming administration had won on a platform of retreating from climate destruction and the oil companies were already figuring out how to divest so their financial damage would be minimal. Still, it would be an historical record of ill gotten gains. Not that most people remembered history because they always repeated it sooner or later.

#   #

It was one of those late in season unbearably hot days that Washington was known for and government all but shut down. The two Daine men were walking, oblivious to the heat. They had buried Yevi, retrieved the papers from the fireplace and almost settled the estate. The house would be donated to one of his dearest friends, another don with a growing family but for now he was continuing to go through the piles of papers written over the years. He could have had it all sent home but once a month he'd gone over to sit in the familiar chair and feel the presence of his best and longest friend who'd been there for him so often. In the end he had failed him but at least he had not known his daughter betrayed him. Bennett had brought home a few souvenirs from their time together, pictures and drinking mugs and his diaries, he would never part with those. A tangled web to be sure, the volatile professor, but he really had been a brother to him.

"I met your mother my last summer at Oxford. She came with an exchange group from Smith College, the prettiest one, by far. All the boys were clearly trying to get her attention and she was nice but more interested in the architecture and history. She loved being there. Naturally, I used that to my advantage, offering to show

245

her around. I had a part time job in the summer office. We gave local tours sometimes and she was really interested. I was totally in love with her before we even spoke. But she was only there for six weeks and there was a lot of competition. Finally, I worked up the nerve to ask her out. I had no money then," he looked around. "Hard to imagine but sometimes wonder if I were happier then, starting out. But I scraped together enough and maybe she knew but she arrived and said she'd had a big lunch and ordered only a salad. So I did, too." He laughed. "I hated salads but I was so taken with her I didn't notice. I was starving by the time I returned to my dorm and out of money." He walked a while, enjoying the memory.

"I don't know how I got the nerve to ask her to marry me. But a few days before she was to leave I just did. She asked why should she marry me? I said, because I'm going to be rich one day. You can have anything you want."

"She smiled and told me, I don't think being rich is a goal. What are you going to do to earn it, rob a bank?"

"No. Currency trading. I've been studying. I think I'll be very good at it. I'll have an investment business. As soon as I graduate I'll seek out capital. My father has some rich friends. I'm sure they'll let me invest some of it for them. When they see I've made them profit, they'll give me more."

"That's a real job?"

"Yes. You'll see. It won't take me long and I'll come to you and propose properly. If you'll wait for me."

Joshua said. "She waited for you."

"I wasn't wealthy right away, of course. My father died soon after and his friends were a little tight, longtime family connections held their money and most had it tied up in their estate. Death duties were killing them. I wasn't sure what to do but I was filled with that blind confidence of youth. Then, almost as if she could read my mind, she wrote and said her father wanted to talk to me about investing. He'd just inherited a decent amount from his parents and she was finished with school. He wanted to save for retirement. I was so excited I think I could have swum across the Atlantic."

Joshua had never seen his father this giddy, no other word for it. He had so few memories of seeing them together. Then a cloud darkened his expression.

"Shortly after you were born, she was diagnosed with uterine cancer. It was treated successfully but we were told no more children. I assured her that was fine and I was adopted, we could do that. We gave some thought to it but she was weak for a while and I was busy starting my company. We were happy, the three of us. You were always running around, excited by everything. One day boats, one day race cars, one day soccer, you wanted to be something new every day when you grew up."

Joshua remembered none of that. He had no happy memories of childhood. Just loneliness.

"We believed it would always be like that. I was becoming successful, even more than I'd bragged. She loved you so much, and me. No one was more perfect, in every way. Always smiling and laughing about something, usually one of your antics. Then the cancer returned, it had spread and nothing either of us or the

247

doctors could do. I brought in the best ones. I remember feeling so helpless, like falling down a deep dark hole with no end. When she left it's as if she took everything inside of me. For that, I'm sorry. She made me promise not to push you, to let you be a boy, let you find your way. She wrote letters every day, as long as she could, one to each of us."

"I never saw any letters."

"I gave them to you. You were angry and started to tear them up. I took them away and saved them. I said you could have them back one day but you never asked. I wasn't sure if they would help or hurt you. I was afraid it would bring up all the pain. I've never been able to read them. I knew what she would say, about going on without her and being happy. I had no intention of being happy, ever again. I was angry, too. Not at her and while we weren't a strongly religious family, her parents wanted a church burial, she'd put it in her Will very clearly. I never went to church again. But what I now realize is I shut you out, too, and that I regret most. You lost a mother. I sent you to boarding school, it was the only way I could let you have a childhood. I was in no condition to do that for you."

The late afternoon sun and the heat was sticky. Each seemed to decide it was enough for today. Edith had made a meal, both she and Gerald were thrilled the men were talking.

"One more thing."

Joshua waited.

"How would you feel about having a stepmother? I want to move back to New York. With Corie's oldest married, the middle one in college and the youngest about to go off, she could use a diversion. We both could. I offered to take her on a long vacation, actually visit a place without thinking of work. I plan to ask her to marry me."

"Personally, I thought you should have married her years ago, banging around here, it was only a matter of time before you started talking to pictures on the wall."

"And you?"

"Some things to work through first."

# #

Valerie rather liked her visits with Dr. Cheng. Even though she was only professionally friendly it had been a while since she'd had real friends, if one can call teenage groupings to discuss boys actual friends. Her time with Famke buying clothes showed her what she was missing; even though the woman earned a commission from her, she'd felt the connection.

Now, with Joshua again doing his disappearing act and no idea when he'd return, if ever, she was feeling the loss. All he'd said on their last meeting, at the hotel, was that he was no longer working as a field agent, time to let others take over, the rules were changing.

She'd thought for a minute he had more to say but all he'd told her was he was going with his father to Oxford.

She'd been cleared of any involvement in Gallagher's death but they would need to get her statement. She'd returned to her old job, tracking money.

Dr. Cheng explained she was here more or less voluntarily, for the final report on fit for duty. S.O.P. She was free to talk about what she wanted. Kellenstone had cleared her but didn't want it to look like a favor, play by the rules, that was Monroe. She smiled. She knew him well as he'd come in often for clarity; he trusted no one else but Midget and she had enough on her plate. Even so, she'd been surprised to learn of his past, she'd known he had secrets kept even from her but then, didn't they all?

So Valerie talked, as she never had. About her childhood and the shame of her father and how she'd been afraid to make friends because they'd always wonder if they could trust her. How she'd missed having a family especially her brother, who ultimately couldn't cope. She hid in her work and thought of Joshua as her family but clearly, he had other ideas.

"How do you feel about that?"

"Alone. But I suppose I always was. Work is okay. I'm trying to fit in more. Derek and I work well together. He took me home to meet his mother, it's just the two of them and we've become friends. I'm not sure he likes that so much, when we get talking he plays video games. We're trying to find him a girlfriend."

Dr. Cheng smiled. "You might want to let him do that on his own."

"You're probably right."

"Anything else?"

"Not really. I think maybe I'll slink back into society. Juliette, my roommate in Paris, just had a baby. Her husband got some notoriety with the money laundering scandal and has been doing quite well and she's a curator at a small museum. They even bought a small flat with a real bedroom and thicker walls. I said I'd come visit, bring Sally, Derek's mom. She's never been to Paris."

"You're doing very well, then. Keep it up. And my door's always open."

"Thank you. Yeah, I feel better, most of the time. If I get lonely I can visit Stockholm. Famke says we can spend the day together, she'll find me a stylish new wardrobe for work."

Dr. Cheng laughed. "I have to admit, that sounds wonderful. Maybe I should take some time for a shopping spree. I just have someone bring over outfits and I pick a few. Good luck."

Valerie now slept soundly. Years in the field had deprived her of long luxurious weekend sleep ins and while she hadn't yet moved from her dingy apartment she had checked out a unit in a nearby luxury high rise but couldn't quite see herself in elevators. A couple of houses within driving distance were way out of her budget. But she had bought a new bed, top of the line and all new linens that matched. Sleep was now her new hobby, bad dreams and adrenaline rush of her job behind her. She no longer drank even wine with dinner and made an effort to eat well, salads for dinner from the farmer's market at the local high school. She hadn't been to the shooting range in months.

From the doorway Joshua stared at her a long time. He knew he'd left her feeling abandoned at the hotel. He'd wanted to tell her so much but it wouldn't come out. He had no idea how she felt about him. He had so many loose ends to tie up with his father that he wasn't yet willing to risk his feelings. Now, watching her sleep, he could see the difference. She'd done really well without him. He couldn't decide if that made him happy for her or sad for himself.

He knew Valerie was back at the desk job, her forensic accounting skills were gaining recognition, they were going to offer her Gallagher's job, permanently, to head up the department. So far, she'd resisted, the actual work was the challenge not nerd herding. She and Derek, too, were growing stars; the little twerp thought he was her new partner. He'd put him in his place soon enough.

He didn't want to wake her. So many times he'd had to grab her and run. Now she could sleep without interruption.

The next day he called Dr. Cheng. Even though the flashbacks had not occurred again he thought she could help him reconcile his past with his future, as head of Daine Investments. His father and Corie were in Greece, Rod in Texas to reconnect with his past, and the O'Leery's had retired to Ireland. He had no one but Valerie and he didn't know how to tell her.

He had agreed, less reluctantly that he'd thought he would be, to oversee his father's business while he was away. Not yet a permanent arrangement but a fresh start, one step at a time, for both of them. He could teach at the academy where he was heralded for his reputation or write a novel loosely based on his experiences or spend all day by the pool or travel to places he'd never been, but none of it appealed to him. Now in his forties and he had literally no idea what he wanted to do with his life.

His father planned to turn the estate into a center for climate control study, dedicated to Yevi, Birkstraach to bring in the right people. It was a stretch to accept his dad's continued loyalty to his friend after all that had happened but it was a worthy cause. He certainly didn't want to live there.

For the first time he realized he didn't have to choose, he had the resources for anything he wanted. That was almost the worst part. Without anger at his father and a need to do the opposite he'd lost his compass. He'd taken to following Valerie, like a stalker. He knew it was wrong but he couldn't help himself.

One day, she stopped at an ice cream store. He'd never seen her eat ice cream. For some reason that upset him. He had no idea what she liked. Now he saw that failure as his, so wrapped up in his own misery he didn't see she might have been as unhappy as he was. She had no family and he'd never tried to fill that gap. He felt too much emotional connection in the field could be deadly. It made them a great team but at what cost?

They weren't in the field now. If he didn't tell her soon he might lose her, she was beginning to move on, he wasn't. As she sat down, prepared to dig into a ridiculously large bowl of multicolored scoops, whipped cream, chocolate sauce dripping all over, he grabbed a spoon from another table and sat, helping himself to a proper gorge.

She looked up. "I was wondering if you were going to follow me forever in case, what, I tripped and you had a band aid? Or you're the food police? Even when I got my hair done, that's perseverance. Then again, you always were the patient one."

"It looks good like that. The color."

"Famke's sister showed me how highlights added brightness to a face."

He looked puzzled. She laughed. "I made a friend. In Stockholm. Two actually. You were…. " Her face clouded, she stuffed a bite in her mouth.

"I know. I'm sorry. My father and I…. there was a lot to do, and talk about. There were some papers… what I mean is, I had more to say to you, too, but… "

"But you're here now. Or did you just come to rescue me from a sugar buzz?" She was sort of smiling; at least she wasn't angry.

He wanted to say she should marry him because he was going to be rich just like his dad. Instead, he said, "You never got ice cream before. You're right, I was hungry. This is really good." He had another spoonful, avoiding her eyes.

"My brother. I miss him. When I'd get in trouble my mother would send me to my room. My brother, his room was near the back staircase, would sneak us out to get ice cream. We returned in such a sugar high, worse than being drunk it is, our mother would send us both to our rooms. It used to infuriate her when we giggled so much at the punishment. I didn't eat it for a long time, it made me sad. Then, at the cabin I reached for it, the most natural thing in the world. Now it brings me happy memories of him. Dr. Cheng said that's when grief moves to acceptance."

He looked surprised at that. "In Stockholm there was this museum, of model trains. I used to love trains as a kid and wanted a set to build but my dad said no, a waste of time. I had to study, get grades, he didn't want me going to Oxford on his name but my own efforts.

254

That seemed all that mattered to him, like I was his reward to show off. But my mother took me, on my birthday. I happened to pass it and went in. Not much like I remembered but I felt close to her, how much she smiled. I wanted to remember her smile and it was hard to think of good times after she left."

They finished the bowl in silence.

"Do you trust me?"

"Not even a little bit."

"You must be up for a vacation."

"I don't like it already."

"Have I ever let you down?"

"Yeah, all the time. How many times have I rescued you?"

"Other than that."

"And maybe let you rescue me once or twice."

"Six times, but who's counting?"

He would ask her to marry him because he was going to be rich just like his dad. Next time, definitely, he would say it out loud.

Meanwhile, there was a nice little house in Stockholm that needed a new ceiling fan, some paint and a woman's touch.

But first, he would take some books and a new winter coat to his young friend Maya. Without her he would have died on that riverbank. Maybe add some college brochures, tell her to study hard. She'd like Oxford, just like his dad.

THE END

Kathy Harter is a Los Angeles based writer with a love of travel. She studied at Oxford and spends time in Stockholm. For more information and other books see her author page
at <u>Amazon.com/author/kathyharter</u>

or Twitter **@kathy_harter**

A Conference in Stockholm in the first in a Stockholm Series trilogy about C.I.A. agents Valerie Rhodes and Joshua Daine. *A House In Stockholm* is the second and *A Meeting in Stockholm* will be out soon.

Other books by Kathy Harter

Fame Can Be Murder
Mac's Wife
Brothers in Name Only
Divorce, Hollywood Style
El Conejo Rides Again

Printed in Great Britain
by Amazon